Marc looked [...]
with such a [...]
have a rema [...]

'Sometimes you make remarks some people would define as sexual harassment,' she said, in a low, tense voice.

'It's outside working hours, Sophie. Tonight you are one of my guests and I'll say what I please... I'm sure you're aware that you have an alluring mouth.'

'I've never been called prim before.'

'Perhaps you aren't...with other men. Perhaps it's only with me that you back off.'

She was forced to stay by his fingers clamping her wrist. As he spoke he shifted his grip, his fingers sliding up from her wrist to enfold her hand. Sophie felt her defences melting like butter in the sun. Surely he couldn't intend to kiss her again?

Anne Weale was still at school when a women's magazine published some of her stories. At twenty-five she had her first novel accepted by Mills & Boon. Now, with a grown-up son and still happily married to her first love, Anne divides her life between her winter home, a Spanish village ringed by mountains and vineyards, and a summer place in Guernsey, one of the many islands around the world she has used as backgrounds for her books.

Recent titles by the same author:

A NIGHT TO REMEMBER

SOPHIE'S SECRET

BY
ANNE WEALE

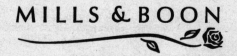

First published in Great Britain 1996
Harlequin Mills & Boon Limited,
Eton House, 18-24 Paradise Road, Richmond, Surrey TW9 1SR

© Anne Weale 1996

ISBN 0 263 79958 1

Set in Times Roman 10 on 11¼ pt.
02-9702-58783 C1

Printed and bound in Great Britain
by Mackays of Chatham PLC, Chatham

CHAPTER ONE

SITTING in the Air France departure lounge for Concorde passengers at New York's Kennedy Airport, Sophie Hill looked as calm and confident as the rest of the cosseted travellers waiting to board their supersonic flight across the Atlantic to Paris.

But her air of relaxed composure was superficial. Inwardly she was tense with excitement and uncertainty.

In her elegant suit and discreetly stylish jewellery, Sophie could easily have passed for a rising star in the legal or banking world, setting out on assignment to Europe. In fact she was a member of the quietly influential network of top people's personal assistants. After starting her career by temping for a large secretarial agency to gain experience, and then working in France for a time, following that with a spell in London, for the past two years she had been PA to a New York insurance broker.

Now she was joining the payroll of someone even more important: the man at the summit of a vast international empire—but a man who kept a low profile and was said to maintain a press relations department to keep his name *out* of the papers.

Sophie had expected to fly business class to Italy. To find herself suddenly transferred to the Concorde flight to Paris had been unexpected, and she still didn't know the reason behind the last-minute change of plan. It seemed that, in addition to paying them exceptionally generous salaries, her new employer treated his worldwide team of personal assistants with unusual consideration.

All the same, she would have felt happier had she been able to meet him before signing the contract to work for him. The position she was taking up had some unexplained aspects that made her faintly uneasy.

She hadn't applied for the job because of its tempting salary. Its location had been the main lure. She would be working in Venice, arguably the most beautiful and romantic city in the world.

Shortly before take-off time, with most of the passengers already boarded, a latecomer entered the Concorde lounge.

Observant by nature and training, Sophie had already cast an interested eye over her fellow passengers, both those who had arrived before her and those who had followed her in. But the man who was pausing to speak to the ground stewardess by the entrance had things about him to catch the eye and the interest of even a less alert woman.

He was very tall and, despite being casually dressed, carried himself with a recognisable air of authority. Most of the men on this flight wore the uniform of chief executives: well-tailored city suits with expensive shirts and shoes, and the costly accessories appropriate to their standing.

The tall man wore cream-coloured trousers, a white shirt, open at the neck, and a single-breasted black jacket with the matt look of fine barathea. While Sophie and all the other passengers had overcoats, raincoats and various other accoutrements, he had brought nothing but a book.

As she watched him speaking to the stewardess, to her astonishment the girl nodded and indicated Sophie. With a word of thanks the tall man turned away from the desk, his stride bringing him swiftly to where she was sitting.

'Good morning, Sophie. I'm Marc Washington.'

Her job had taught her to maintain an appearance of unflappability in the face of almost any contingency. Even so, to be confronted by her new employer in these circumstances was the last thing she had anticipated and a severe test of her self-possession. She passed it, but only by a whisker.

'Good morning, Mr Washington. I wasn't expecting to meet you here.'

'Having to cope with the unexpected is one of the elements of working for me,' he replied as they shook hands. 'The flight is an opportunity for us to get acquainted. Shall we...?' The unfinished question was accompanied by a gesture in the direction of the boarding tunnel.

After stooping to pick up her bag, her book and her lightweight raincoat, she accompanied him across the lounge, her own height of five feet eight dwarfed by his much taller frame.

Although she had not had long to take in his features full face, her mind retained an impression of dark eyes under black eyebrows and a naturally olive skin still deepened by a summer tan.

But, of course, for a man of his means sunlight was available all year. Although he might have to spend much of his time in capital cities where winter brought bad weather, weekends at ski resorts or sailing from sunlit marinas would not, for him, be a rare treat. They would be frequent occurrences.

Somehow, with not much to go on, she had assumed Marc Washington would be a middle-aged workaholic, obsessed by high finance and complex power games. But he looked to be still in his thirties, with the physique of a man who kept fit in pleasurable ways—not, like her previous boss, by working out on machines in an expensive downtown gymnasium because his physician advised it.

From talking to other PAs whose bosses used Concorde regularly, Sophie knew the most coveted seats were the four at the front, often occupied by royalty. Today, two of these seats had been kept for Marc Washington and herself.

As a stewardess in a double-buttoned deep blue dress took her raincoat away Sophie couldn't help wondering if her name would have been memorised had she been travelling alone, instead of as the companion of a man whose name might not appear in the newspapers but was sure to be flagged as a VIP on the database of regular Concorde users.

Assuming he would prefer the window seat, although the window was smaller and higher than on a subsonic aircraft, she stood aside for him to precede her into their seat space. But he shook his head and gestured for her to go first.

As she sat down and fastened the seat belt across her hips, the sight of her knees reminded Sophie of one of the key qualifications required in candidates for the job she had won. Great legs.

That proviso, with its sexist implications, had almost put her off applying. But the prospect of working in Venice had overcome her disquiet that Marc Washington might expect more than secretarial services from the women he employed to smooth his working life.

Now, because he was younger than she had expected, and gave an immediate impression of powerful virility, her unease resurfaced. Was he going to expect her to be his playgirl by night as well as his PA by day?

In general Sophie took a relaxed view of the natural hazards of being a presentable female. Perhaps she had been lucky. So far the men she had worked with had not been the kind who made unwelcome passes.

But the man settling his broad shoulders against the backrest next to hers was a totally unknown quantity. He might be a macho type who saw the entire female sex as an extended harem from which he could select whoever took his fancy and expect an amenable response.

If he thought that because he was paying her an exceptionally high salary he was entitled to everything she had to give, he could think again. In Sophie's view the duties of a PA went a long way beyond those of most employees in terms of time and support. They didn't include the kind of personal attentions he might have in mind.

Not, to be fair to him, that Marc Washington was giving the female cabin staff the once-over like the elderly lecher seated across the aisle. Her new employer seemed unaware that a great pair of legs belonging to one of the stewardesses was in close-up view while its owner spoke to another member of the cabin staff. He was arranging his own long legs.

Sophie chose to keep hers angled out of sight, apart from a few inches of black-hosed knees exposed by the hem of the black skirt which went with the black and cream plaid jacket and cream silk shirt she had chosen to travel in.

In her working life she strove to emulate the understated chic of top career women ten years her senior. The colours she loved, and which matched her large blue-green eyes, were confined to her scarf and underwear drawers and to the contents of the jewellery roll now in her capacious travelling bag.

Although it seemed unlikely that any Concorde passengers would be suffering from pre-flight nerves, they were offered champagne before take-off.

'Not for me, thank you,' she said with a smile, when the steward presented the tray to her. 'But I would like a glass of water...when you have time.'

'You don't like champagne, or you don't drink alcohol at all?' Marc Washington asked her after the steward had passed by, leaving him holding a glass of the gently fizzing wine.

'On the contrary, with pasta suppers at my New York neighbourhood trattoria I always drank my share of the carafe of house wine,' she answered. Impulsively she added, 'To be honest, I'm on a stratospheric high already...what with being on the way to Venice and the surprise of finding myself flying Concorde.'

Marc Washington's mouth didn't alter but his eyes did. Suddenly they gleamed with amusement.

'I'm glad to hear it,' he said as the supersonic aircraft rose from the ground. 'Your composure suggested otherwise. I have a powerful thirst for life, Sophie, and I like the people around me to feel the same way. My impression, when we shook hands, was of someone noticeably guarded in their responses. It didn't tally with Audrey LaRue's impression that you were exactly right for the Venetian assignment.'

'That's good to hear,' said Sophie. 'I wanted the job very much and I'm looking forward to starting it. Mrs LaRue explained that liaising with the Venetian civic authorities would be an important part of it, but beyond that I know very little.'

'That's why we're travelling together, so that I can explain it to you. Your dossier says you've been to Venice before. How long did you spend there?'

This was a question Sophie wanted to sidestep. To answer it fully would be painful to her, and anyway the whole truth was none of his business.

She said, 'Longer than the majority of tourists who, so I read, spend an average of sixteen hours there. I know the city a little better than they do, but not as well as I'd like to.'

Fortunately her answer seemed to satisfy him. 'By the time my project is accomplished you'll know it well,' he assured her. 'I hope the problems you're going to have to deal with won't spoil the place for you.'

'I'm sure they won't. What sort of problems will they be?'

As she spoke they were handed menus.

'Before I go into that, let's decide what to eat.'

For some seconds, as he fixed his attention on the dishes listed on the card, she was able to study his face more closely than had been possible until now.

As a small child she had been taught to give close attention to the structure of people's faces, to observe how their mouths drooped or curled, to notice how features varied and to read the signs revealing a person's character.

'Faces are maps...maps of experience and temperament.' She remembered the voice and the remark as clearly as if she had heard it yesterday.

What kind of man and what kind of life was mapped in Marc Washington's face? She found it impossible to tell. She could recognise his charisma but she couldn't begin to guess what lay behind it. At this stage of their acquaintance he was a complete enigma.

Working for him would change that. The old French quote 'No man is a hero to his valet' could nowadays be updated to, No man is a mystery to his PA.

Her last boss had been a nice man with a stable marriage and no affairs on the side. At present she didn't even know if Marc Washington had a wife, an ex-wife or two, or a succession of girlfriends.

When a stewardess came to take their orders for lunch, Sophie asked for curried apricot and mint soup followed by a nest of quail's eggs with an asparagus salad and, for pudding, poached pears in red wine fruit jelly.

Marc Washington's choices were more robust. He had decided to start with oysters, followed by saddle of hare in a mustard sauce with several vegetables. He concluded his order with the three-layer chocolate mousse.

'Did your friends give you a send-off at that West Side trattoria you party at?'

As she hadn't mentioned the restaurant's location she concluded he must remember the address from her dossier. If his memory was as retentive as that, she would have to be doubly sure she never forgot any details.

She smiled at him. 'Yes, they did. I made some good friends during my time in America. I'm glad I crossed the Atlantic, but I'm glad to be going back to Europe.'

At this point their meal began. A week or two earlier Sophie's ex-boss had received a brochure about the Air France Concorde. She had read it, never expecting to travel on it. Recently the interior of the aircraft had been redesigned by the internationally famous André Putman, whose approach to design was simplicity rather than ostentatious luxury.

Sophie had already noticed that the headrest covers were of crisp white cotton piqué protecting a subdued upholstery of finely ribbed grey and beige wool. The tablecloths had hem-stitched edges, the starkly simple white china was narrowly rimmed with blue, and the cutlery was presented in a roll of corrugated paper tied with a matching cord. It was all a far cry from the garish colours and emphasis on synthetics of most airlines. Clearly Marc Washington took all this elegance for granted. Perhaps he had never experienced any other kind of in-flight meal.

As she dipped her spoon in her soup the memory of the horrible refreshments on a cut-price flight to Mexico, where she and her friend Merle had spent Christmas, made Sophie smile inwardly. Yet, even after that uncomfortable flight, perhaps they had enjoyed themselves as much as these Concorde passengers at their five-star resorts or in their luxurious houses.

As it seemed her companion preferred to enjoy his oysters in silence, she didn't speak while they ate. Out of the corner of her eye she could see the leisurely movements of his long fingers and the light catching the glass and metal of the watch protruding from the edge of his white shirt-cuff.

It wasn't an ostentatious watch, nor, although they were well kept, were his nails professionally manicured, she noticed. But in a line-up of all the expensively tailored, smoothly groomed men on this aircraft he would stand out for many reasons.

As she often did, she heard an echo from the past. 'Don't be a conformist, Sophie. Don't run with the herd. Go your own way.'

But she had conformed. With her living to earn and no special talents to take her in a different direction, there had been no option but to join the big city rat-race.

While she was admiring her next course, a pale golden hollandaise sauce coating four quail's eggs and overflowing their nest of puff pastry and puréed broccoli, her new employer broke his silence.

'One of the best eggs I ever ate was a bantam's, fried in olive oil, topping a sliver of mountain ham on a chunk of village bread,' he said reminiscently. 'It came with a glass of brandy on a very cold morning.'

'Somewhere in Italy?'

'No, in a scruffy little *pueblo* in the mountains of southern Spain. I'd been to the Sierra Nevada to see the world ski championships, but they had to be cancelled for lack of snow. So I spent a few days exploring the Alpujarra region.'

The way his tongue rolled the 'r's in the Spanish name made Sophie suspect he spoke the language. In her experience it was unusual for Americans to be linguists, unless their parents or grandparents had been immigrants. Those whose forebears had come to America a long time ago tended, like the British, to expect everyone to speak their language.

'Are you a polyglot, Mr Washington?' she asked.

'I wish I were. I have a few words of several languages but I'm only fluent in Italian...which means I can get by in Spain. What made you choose Italian as your principal language?'

'When I was small, someone in my family spoke it. I used to like listening to them...I still think it's the most musical language in Europe.' In case he should press for a fuller explanation, she said, 'You were going to tell me some of the problems I'll have to deal with.'

'First I'll explain the project. When you visited Venice, did you go to any of the other islands in the lagoon— Torcello—Burano—Murano?'

When she nodded, he went on, 'Those three are the only ones most tourists see, but there are more than thirty. The cost of saving Venice for posterity is immense. No other city in the world has so many historic buildings and no other city has its foundations in the sea. To raise more money for the preservation of Venice an auction was held for long low-rent leases on thirteen of the unused islands in the lagoon. I was one of the successful bidders. My island is called Capolavoro.'

'What are you planning to do with it?' she asked.

'It's going to become a refuge.'

'For wildlife?'

'For me. My present base in Venice is the top floor of a *palazzo* built by my mother's family. The rest of it's home to various elderly relations. I need somewhere quieter and more private.'

'I hadn't realised you were yourself a Venetian on your mother's side,' said Sophie.

Although now, looking at him with that knowledge, she wondered why she hadn't guessed that his forebears included some of the extraordinary men who had made their fortunes in Venice and spent them on the magnificent palaces along the Grand Canal.

Rogues and schemers, many of them, some cruel and ruthless in achieving their objectives, all of them had been motivated by the powerful thirst for life he had warned her he had and expected his underlings to share.

Suddenly Sophie had the feeling that she might be out of her depth, that working for Marc Washington would be unlike any previous job and, in spite of the laudatory references given her by previous employers, she might not have the skills to cope with the man beside her.

All this went through her mind in seconds, leaving only a brief pause before she went on, 'Where do you feel you belong . . . in Venice or America?'

Having asked, she wished she hadn't. He might think the question too inquisitive.

'I belong wherever I am,' he said. 'There aren't many parts of the global village where I haven't been or where I feel out of place.'

She had already noticed that while he talked he looked intently at her, never switching his gaze somewhere else as most people did when conversing.

'Where do you feel you belong?' he asked. 'In that little village in Devon where you were born?'

He really did have a phenomenal recall of facts, thought Sophie, switching her own gaze to the bulkhead in front of her. To remember the county of her birthplace was remarkable, and how did he know it was a village with a population of fewer than five hundred people? Perhaps Mrs LaRue had checked, adding a note to Sophie's dossier.

'No, definitely not,' she answered. 'I was there for six months as a baby and then taken somewhere else. The place where I belong is somewhere I haven't found yet.'

The meal was over and they were drinking coffee when Marc Washington said, 'Once you've been shown the ropes, I shall have to leave you to handle things on your own a great deal of the time, although you'll always be able to contact me. Your role will be to liaise with all the people involved in the restoration and development of Capolavoro. To be a mediator when they come into conflict—as they will.'

'May I ask you why you didn't engage a home-grown PA for this?'

'That was my first intention, but no one good enough applied. In Italy top-level PAs gravitate to Milan and Rome. Anyway, there are advantages in bringing in an outsider. In many ways Italy is one of the most civilised countries in the world, but getting things done quickly and efficiently has always been a problem,' he said drily. 'Americans are better at that. I was expecting all the New York applicants to be American.'

Sophie couldn't resist asking, 'What gave me the edge over the two other finalists?'

'In terms of qualifications you were very evenly matched. In that situation the choice depends on the selector's quirks. I liked the look of you best,' he added casually.

For a second or two she was flattered. Then, slightly perplexed, she said, 'But we didn't submit photographs. When did you see us?'

'While you were in the waiting room. The Venetian mirror you noticed when you came in is also a one-way window.'

'A window!' Sophie's startled exclamation drew a glance from a passing stewardess.

'The fact that you were the only one to appreciate the nature of the frame was a minor point in your favour. I like people who take an interest in their surroundings and recognise fine things.'

'You've ruined the fineness of that mirror by replacing the proper glass with that nasty piece of one-way window glass,' Sophie informed him bluntly.

Normally she had a low boiling point, and had not lost her temper in years. But anger welled up in her now and she couldn't contain it.

'I think watching people without their knowing it is...' On the brink of saying unpardonable, she modified her word to, 'Unethical.'

'But practical,' he said coolly. 'More revealing than a face-to-face meeting when you would have been putting on a front. I saw you behaving naturally.'

'Could you hear what we were saying?'

'No, the room isn't bugged.'

His indifference to her disapproval fanned her anger. 'You surprise me,' she said sarcastically. 'If you're prepared to spy on people, why jib at listening?'

'You exaggerate. Watching people and even, in certain circumstances, listening to them, isn't the same as spying on them. It's an accepted technique which has many applications. Manufacturing companies often use it to gauge customers' reactions to their product. They set up consumer discussion groups and listen to them talking. The groups know they're being monitored but they respond more freely without the visible presence of people taking notes.'

'That's the difference...they *know*. We didn't. We thought you weren't in the building. Didn't it cross your mind that we had a right to see *you*?'

She knew she was taking a tone he wouldn't like, but she felt impelled to have this out with him. It was a matter of principle.

'If you had met me, would it have made you withdraw your application?' he asked sardonically.

The arrogance implicit in his question brought a crisp retort from Sophie. 'I already had reservations about it. I might well have withdrawn if I'd known about the mirror. I'm sure Mrs LaRue can't have liked being a party to that. I thought she looked uncomfortable when she told us you wouldn't be able to see us.'

'Audrey may not be comfortable with a lot of my methods but she knows which side her bread is buttered. If you can't accept my authority, if you're going to purse your lips every time I do something you don't like, it had better be hello and goodbye. You can fly back from Paris at my expense and I'll send for one of the other two.'

A stewardess removed their empty coffee-cups. When she was out of earshot, he said, 'Think it over. I don't want anyone working for me who can't go along with the way I do things. I'm going to read now. You have the rest of the flight to decide.'

CHAPTER TWO

FOR a while Sophie sat silently simmering, but gradually her temper cooled. She realised she had handled the whole thing very badly. When she'd found out about the mirror, she should have held her tongue until she'd had time to think it over.

This way, by speaking recklessly, she had diminished her credit with him if she did decide to stay with the job.

Now, from the window, Sophie could see the curvature of the earth and the infinity of space. It was only by courtesy of the man beside her that she was having this experience. Many people would think her crazy to put at risk the salary and the opportunities that working for him offered.

Later in the flight, while they were still in the stratosphere at their cruising altitude, he suddenly closed his book, adjusted the angle of his seat and lay back and shut his eyes. She thought he was probably thinking rather than sleeping, although there were many examples of famously dynamic men who topped up their energy with catnaps.

Either way, he looked subtly different; the angular architecture of his face was softened by the closed eyelids and unexpectedly silky black eyelashes near the downward slash of his cheekbones. When his eyes were open, the probing scrutiny of his Italian-dark irises distracted attention from his eyelashes.

She was thinking about the strange mixture of his bloodlines—old Virginian and even older Venetian—

19

when she had the strangest feeling that somewhere, a long time ago, she had seen him before.

Where?

Reviewing all the cities where their paths could have crossed or converged, if only for a few moments in some expensive street where she had been window-shopping and he had been buying, she failed to come up with an answer.

In one year, if you worked in a city, you saw thousands of faces, she thought. Did the brain memorise all those images, stashing them away in the back of the mind, most of them irrecoverable but a few in a special place from which they could be retrieved like the hidden files on a computer?

What she did remember, very clearly, was the evening this adventure had begun. Not that she had immediately recognised it as a turning point. Did one ever? she thought, her mind going back to the evening in question.

'So what's new in your world?' asked Merle.

After watching fifteen minutes of the news they had agreed to zap the newscast and eat their lap-suppers in peace.

Sophie shrugged. 'Nothing much.'

She was in her white terry bathrobe which, according to Merle, made her look at least ten years younger than twenty-five. Especially with her face cleansed with mousse, and her blonde hair, normally worn in a sleek, swingy bob, caught up by a tortoiseshell spring-clip from which a few silky tendrils had escaped to curl round her ears and her high cheekbones, which had emerged from the round, cheerful face captured in photographs of her schooldays.

Both her job and Merle's involved working late several nights a week. Tonight Sophie had got home in time to take a quick shower before fixing a salad to go with the fillets of salmon she had slipped under the grill when she'd heard a key in the lock of their shared West Side apartment.

'How did your day go?' she asked Merle now.

Having just filled her mouth with salad, her friend waved her fork to signal that she would reply in a moment. Like Sophie she was a PA, her boss being the founder of New York's most famous firm of headhunters.

Most of the people they hunted were senior executives required for plum positions with America's commercial giants. But sometimes they searched for people lower down the corporate scale, even recruiting secretaries when exceptional skills were asked for.

When Merle could speak, she said, 'Something came in today I wouldn't have minded trying for myself if my CV had filled the bill. Whoever lands this cushy number has to speak fluent Italian. I only have French.'

'Why is Italian a must?' asked Sophie.

'The job is in Venice, Italy.'

When Sophie had been working in London, before crossing the Atlantic, it had puzzled her that Americans always said 'Paris, France' or 'Naples, Italy'. Soon after arriving in New York she had realised that almost every town and city in Europe had a namesake, and sometimes several, in the United States.

Any mention of what, to her, was the one and only Venice always triggered her interest. She never spoke of the reasons why the Italian city was special to her, but even to see on a poster in the window of a travel agency the familiar bow-prong of a gondola, or one of the famous bridges over the network of canals, was enough to revive poignant memories.

'What is the job?' she asked.

'Same as yours,' Merle replied. 'PA to a boss who expects to have a miracle-worker in his outer office. But he's ready to pay big bucks for his wonder woman.'

Sophie's eyes widened when Merle told her the salary the job carried. 'Every PA in New York with a smattering of Italian will be lining up for an interview,' she went on. 'But, aside from being genuinely fluent, there are some other essentials that will whittle the final line-up down to single figures.'

'What are the other qualifications?' Sophie asked, aware that she was beginning to feel more than a casual interest.

For some months now she had been waking up in the morning without the sense of eagerness to see what the coming day offered that she felt people ought to experience if their life was on the right track.

New York, so exciting and stimulating when she had first come here, had begun to lose some of its charm— in the same way that London had palled after a few years of working there.

Maybe she was growing out of big cities, beginning to need a different kind of environment. But what and where was a puzzle she had yet to solve.

'For a start the successful applicant has to be free of all ties,' said Merle. 'No husband, no partner, no one she's serious about.'

'That's not going to thin out the field much,' Sophie said drily. 'This city is teeming with women who would sell their souls to have a man in their life. But the only ones they ever meet are other women's husbands or their discards. Neither of us has a guy we couldn't bear to tear ourselves away from. Will we ever?' she added, with a faint sigh.

Merle said, 'You could have plenty of dates if you were less picky. I couldn't see too much wrong with Robert.'

'There wasn't anything wrong with him,' Sophie agreed. 'He just didn't make me feel the way people should if they're going to spend the rest of their lives together.'

'That's an ideal that doesn't work out in real life,' Merle said firmly.

Sophie knew that Merle thought her views naïve and unrealistic for a person in her mid-twenties; she had already abandoned a couple of promising relationships for reasons which didn't make sense to her friend's way of thinking.

They had argued the subject many times, and sometimes, awake in the night, Sophie wondered if Merle was right and her expectations *were* set too high.

Now, to avoid another disagreement, she recapped the qualifications Merle had already mentioned. 'Fluent Italian. No ties. What else?'

'Great legs.'

'You're kidding!'

Sophie had lived in America long enough to know what an uproar *that* requirement would cause in certain quarters. Even in Europe, where the feminist and politically correct lobbies were not yet as powerful as here, it would be considered unacceptably sexist for a male employer to insist on specific physical attributes in his female employees.

'We're not advertising that,' said Merle. 'But, although we're keeping it quiet, only the long-stemmed applicants will get through to the final interview.'

'This client must have a lot of clout to get away with that proviso. Who is he?' Sophie asked.

'No one you've ever heard of—but with as much clout, if not more, than most of the top tycoons who *are* household names,' Merle told her. 'His name is Marc Washington . . . the Marc spelt with a c.'

In Sophie's job it was essential to read and absorb information from all the best sources of international business news. If asked, she could have given a résumé on most of the financial and commercial top people. But her mental file didn't come up with any facts about Marc Washington.

The following day she asked her boss about him. It turned out that Washington was the heir to a fortune founded in the last century by a man with ancestral links to the Virginian family whose most famous son had been America's first president. However, although Marc Washington was known to have a finger in many successful pies, he was a mysterious figure about whose personal life little was known outside his immediate circle.

From then on, each evening, Sophie couldn't resist asking Merle how the search for someone to fill the Venetian post was progressing.

'Why are you so interested?' Merle asked, about a week later.

Sophie's answer surprised them both. Until that moment she hadn't made up her mind to take such a life-changing step.

'I'd like to apply for the job, Merle.'

Merle took a minute or two to recover from her surprise. Eventually she said, 'You fit the bill on most counts, including the great legs. But the key qualification is the fluent Italian.'

'I speak Italian as well as you speak French.'

'You do? Why didn't you tell me?'

'It never came up.'

After a pause, Merle said, 'There's quite a lot about you that's never come up, isn't there, Sophie? I've always known there were parts of your life you didn't want to talk about, and I've gone along with that, but the applicants for this job have to fill in a long questionnaire giving their entire life history. Are you prepared to do that?'

'If I want the job, I'll have to, won't I?' Sophie responded lightly.

Inwardly, she had no intention of revealing every aspect of her past to an employer whose own life was shrouded in secrecy.

On the day of the final interview Sophie already knew that only seven people had survived the preliminary sifting. Those on the short-list had then been re-interviewed by the charming but eagle-eyed woman who was Marc Washington's personal assistant in New York.

Afterwards, Sophie felt sure she wouldn't be among the finalists bidden to attend an interview with Marc Washington himself. To her surprise, she was.

After taking great care with her appearance, she arrived for the ultimate test to find she had only two rivals. Both were so poised and stylish that she didn't feel she had a hope of being the one chosen by the exacting Mr Washington.

The three of them were introduced to each other by Mrs LaRue, who had conducted the penultimate interviews. Although in her early fifties, Mrs LaRue still had 'great legs', Sophie noticed as the older woman showed them to a comfortably furnished waiting room.

'Mr Washington has been delayed. He expects to arrive very soon,' she said, before leaving them together.

Although none of the three would have been in their present jobs if they hadn't been friendly young women adept at getting along with other people, in this situation their natural warmth was under constraint.

It was Sophie who broke the ice. 'Are you both native New Yorkers? I came here from London a couple of years ago.'

'I'm from Milwaukee,' said Amanda, a willowy brunette with designer glasses framing her long-lashed dark eyes.

Eileen, a freckled redhead, told them she came from Boston, but her colouring suggested that Ireland was where her forebears had originated.

For about fifteen minutes the three of them made somewhat forced conversation. Amanda was the most restive. She prowled the room, looking without much interest at the pictures on the walls, bending to sniff one of the roses in the arrangement of fresh flowers on a side table, and finally selecting a copy of *Vogue* from the low centre table and sitting down to glance through its glossy pages.

Of the three of them, Eileen had the best legs, Sophie considered. But she also had an irritating habit of picking at her nails. Perhaps she was only doing it because she was nervous and would control it while she was being interviewed.

'I wonder who'll go in first?' said Amanda. She had put *Vogue* back on the table and now jumped up to inspect her reflection in a large mirror with an ornate glass frame.

It had been the first thing Sophie had noticed when they'd entered the room because the ornamental frame was typically Venetian, instantly recognisable to anyone who had ever seen one before. But, while the frame was antique and very beautiful, the original glass, which would have made it worth many thousands of dollars, had been replaced by a piece of modern glass.

Mrs LaRue reappeared.

'I'm sorry, ladies. I'm afraid it won't be possible for Mr Washington to see you this afternoon after all. Something has come up that requires his immediate attention. He's asked me to apologise to you.'

'When will he be able to see us?' Amanda asked, frowning.

'That I can't say at the moment. I'll be in touch as soon as possible.' Mrs LaRue's expression and tone were sympathetic.

Sophie had an intuitive feeling that, inwardly, she was annoyed with her employer for messing them about in this way. Perhaps he was a difficult person to work for, with little thought for other people's convenience as long as his own was never interfered with.

Going down to street-level in the elevator, the other two had some pithy comments to make.

'I'm beginning to wonder if I really want this job,' said Amanda. 'The salary is what grabbed me. I'm not crazy to spend time in Venice. I was there on honeymoon with my ex. The shops were better in Rome.'

They parted at the entrance on Sixth Avenue, the other two diving into cabs, leaving Sophie to saunter home in a mood of anticlimax. Merle was out that evening at a party given by a former colleague who was now married.

Sophie found herself pacing the apartment's living room as restlessly as Amanda had prowled the waiting room. She had hoped by this evening to know where she stood instead of being still in suspense.

She was eating her solitary supper when the telephone rang.

'Hello? Sophie Hill speaking.'

'This is Audrey LaRue, Ms Hill. Mr Washington has decided that it won't be necessary to put you to the trouble of attending a further interview.'

Sophie's heart sank with disappointment.

'After studying your CV and my report of the talk we had last week, Mr Washington has decided you are the candidate best qualified to fill the position in Venice.'

'Oh... Oh, that's wonderful!' Sophie exclaimed, her spirits soaring. 'When does he want me to start?'

It was only after they had concluded their conversation that she realised that, while Mr Washington had Mrs LaRue's opinion of her to go on, she knew little more about him than she had at the outset.

It might be that when they did meet she would take an instant dislike to him...

Marc opened his eyes five minutes before they were due to land. Instantly alert to his surroundings and aware of his last words to her, he said, 'Made up your mind?'

Sophie took a deep breath. 'I'll come to Venice.'

'Good.' He pressed the service button and, when the steward came, asked for a glass of water. 'Would you like one, Sophie?'

'Please.'

They were both drinking iced spring water in crystal tumblers when Concorde touched down at Charles de Gaulle Airport where the time was forty-five minutes past ten in the evening. They had been in the air for less than four hours.

When Sophie had queried being re-routed via Paris when her previous Alitalia ticket had been for a flight direct to Venice, Mrs LaRue had merely said, 'Overnight accommodation in Paris has been arranged for you, and a car will take you to and from the city.'

At the time Sophie had been baffled by these arrangements. Merle's reaction had been, 'Go with the flow, honey. If they're picking up the bills, why should you worry?'

In the back of the limousine taking them from the airport to the city centre, Marc said, 'I have an engagement this evening and two meetings tomorrow. But I'm sure you can amuse yourself. We'll fly out first thing the day after tomorrow in my plane. It was grounded with technical trouble after I flew in last week, but the problem has been fixed.'

Some years earlier Sophie had worked for some wine-shippers in Bordeaux to perfect her French. The MD had flown his own plane around south-western France but had never undertaken long flights such as crossing the Swiss Alps between Paris and Venice.

As if he could read her thoughts, Marc said, 'Don't worry, my pilot is very experienced. I have a pilot's licence myself, but I shan't be at the controls tomorrow.'

When they reached central Paris, she expected to be dropped off at a modest hotel before he drove on to one of the *grand luxe* establishments. When the car came to a halt outside an imposing entrance and a liveried doorman opened the nearside rear door, Marc stepped out first, then turned and waited for her to follow.

As they entered the building he said, 'As I'm often in Paris, I have a suite here in preference to an apartment. If you go to the desk, they'll show you to your room. We'll have dinner together tomorrow night. Tonight I suggest you have something light in your room and watch a movie on television. They're usually quite soporific. By the morning you'll have adjusted to European time.'

He turned away in the direction of the lift.

CHAPTER THREE

ALTHOUGH she rarely bought clothes on impulse, preferring to stick to a carefully thought out plan, the next day Sophie fell for a top she saw displayed in a window. It matched her eyes but, in terms of cost per wear, would take for ever to earn its keep in her wardrobe. She couldn't resist it.

Walking back to the hotel, swinging the elegant carrier bag, she knew she had bought it partly on the assumption that she would be dining with Marc in an ambience demanding something more exciting than the cream silk shirt she was wearing again today or the black silk standby in her overnight case.

When she collected her key from the desk, the hall porter handed her a message scrawled on one of the hotel's elegant note slips: 'Bring a wrap. We'll be eating out. M.W.'

She could take her silk-look raincoat. A better option would be the black cashmere shawl packed in her hold luggage. *That* had been a sensible buy, expensive but endlessly wearable. Retrieving it from her suitcase involved finding a pair of scissors to cut the band of security tape which had been on the case when it appeared on the carousel. The shawl was at the bottom of the case. As she unpacked and repacked Sophie chided herself for going to these lengths to dine with her boss.

When, later, she went downstairs and saw that the large, softly lit bar was now full of elegant people, she was glad she had taken the trouble. She remembered reading somewhere that, as well as this hotel being a

home from home to the world's rich, its bar was also a
fashionable early evening rendezvous for Parisians.

A man in a dinner jacket was standing just inside the
bar. Evidently he was staff as he gave her a slight bow,
saying in English, 'Mr Washington is waiting for you at
a table in the corner, *mademoiselle*. Permit me...' He
conducted her through the crowded room.

Marc rose from a velvet banquette when he saw them
coming. In place of yesterday's casual clothes he was
wearing a dark blue striped suit and a pale blue shirt.
Its white collar emphasised his tan. His tie was plain
dark blue silk. His elegance made her glad she had
bought the chic top.

'Thank you.' She smiled at the man who had led her
to him.

Almost before she had sat down a waiter was there to
attend to them. Marc hadn't ordered yet. He had been
reading a French paper.

'What would you like?'

Out of the past came a memory of a voice saying,
'Spritz al bitter, per favore,' and of a glass filled with
deep pink liquid shining in the evening light on the wide,
busy waterfront of the Riva degli Schiavoni.

'May I have a Campari spritzer?'

Marc looked at the waiter. 'I'll have the same... and
some *croustades*, please.' Turning to her, he asked, 'What
did you do with yourself today?'

'Nothing special...just enjoyed Paris. It was too warm
and sunny to be inside a museum.'

'No shopping?'

'No intentional shopping. I did buy one thing that
caught my eye.'

'This?' He indicated her top.

'How did you guess?'

'It looks French. Also, women like to wear something new as soon as possible.' Knowledge of how many women had contributed to that statement? she wondered.

'Did your meetings go well?'

'Yes, our French operation—sports equipment—goes from strength to strength. It started with a small company in which my grandfather invested before other people foresaw the masses enjoying activities that, in his day, were exclusive to the idle rich. Now we have sports supermarts in the commercial section of every large city in France.'

He was talking about the latest developments in the manufacture of indoor climbing walls when their drinks arrived, accompanied by a silver dish, its contents hidden in the folds of a white linen napkin embroidered with the hotel's monogram.

'We'll go out to eat,' said Marc. 'I don't care for the dining room here. The food's good but the atmosphere's dull. When I don't want to go out, I dine in my suite.' As he spoke he picked up his glass, removing the olive from it. 'But as you're already rather tense about working for me I won't suggest we do that this evening.'

His eyes, amused, held hers while he drank.

Sophie wondered if he was testing her, wanting to find out how she would cope with flirtation. She broke their eye contact, taking the olive on its stick out of the pink-tinted mixture of wine and soda.

'I haven't tasted Campari since I was in Italy,' she said, after sipping it. 'What time do we take off tomorrow?'

'Early. The car will be here at seven-thirty. You can breakfast at seven, if you like—room service is very efficient—or on the plane. I always run before breakfast. Tomorrow I'll have my coffee and croissants with Werner after take-off. He used to fly for Lufthansa but got tired of the same long-haul routes. Flying for me is more interesting, and often his wife, Lisa, comes with us.'

Sophie was eating her olive. After swallowing it, she asked, 'Is Lisa also German?'

'Australian. She's the daughter of one of our executives in Sydney and her parents would have preferred her to marry someone local. She's a useful person to have around. She was a nurse until Werner walked into her life. I don't know how the arrangement will work out when they have children, but she's only twenty-three so they're not in a hurry to start a family.'

This gave Sophie a cue to ask, 'Do you have children, Mr Washington?'

'No.'

For a moment she thought he was going to leave it at that and wondered if she was being snubbed because he regarded his private life as off limits.

Then he added, 'Like you, I have no "hostages to fortune". . . if you know that expression.'

'"He that hath wife and children hath given hostages to fortune; for they are impediments to great enterprises, either of virtue or mischief",' Sophie quoted. 'Written by Frances Bacon in his essay *Of Marriage and Single Life*. We did his essays in my last year at school.'

'Do you agree with his view?' After unfolding the napkin, he offered her the dish of *croustades*.

Sophie had eaten them before, during her time in Bordeaux, and had sometimes made them herself when she and Merle had given a party.

'Thank you.' Taking one of the crisp golden curls of bread, spread with butter and Roquefort cheese and sprinkled with caraway seeds, she bit into it with care, trying not to scatter crumbs on her black skirt.

'We could use some napkins.' Before helping himself Marc looked around for the waiter. Having beckoned him, he said, 'Until one arrives, use this.' Taking the silk handkerchief from his breast pocket, he spread it across her lap.

She had already noticed the rich but subtle colours in the overflow of silk, wondering if it might have come from a shop in Venice where once she had feasted her eyes on wonderful ties and handkerchiefs costing hundreds of thousands of lire.

Since breakfast she had had only soft drinks and coffee in a couple of pavement cafés, sitting in the warm end-of-summer sunshine, watching the passing scene. The *croustade* tasted deliciously cheesy. She hadn't realised till then how hungry she was.

When the waiter brought two small napkins she returned Marc's handkerchief. As he stuffed it carelessly back in place she said, 'In sixteenth-century England a wife would have been an impediment to a man who wanted, for example, to explore the New World. But now that women are included in space missions and a British girl has walked the length of Africa there's no reason why a wife should be an impediment to virtuous enterprises. As for impeding mischief, she has never done that if her husband is the promiscuous type.'

Marc moved the dish closer to her side of the table. 'I have a longer reach. Help yourself. They're good, aren't they? Although not, for my taste, quite as good as Italian *crostini* hot from the oven on a cold winter morning. What time of year were you in Venice before?'

Her answer was not exactly a lie, but it came perilously close. 'This time of year.'

He said, 'I like Venice under snow, or shrouded in mist, when the only foreigners around either work there or are in love with the place. When I was small, but old enough to explore on my own, there wasn't a camera or camcorder round every damn corner between the Piazza and the Rialto. It's a vicious circle: without the hordes,

Venice wouldn't survive, but their presence makes parts of the city horribly overcrowded.'

Between them they finished the *croustades*. By the time she emptied her glass, his had been empty for some minutes.

'Would you like another drink?'

'Not for me, but please go ahead if you would.'

'In that case, let's go and do some serious eating.'

Midway through dinner Sophie realised this was the best evening out she had had in a long time. They were in a neighbourhood restaurant on the Left Bank. It was not unlike her favourite West Side place. Here, as there, it was run by a family—the parents sharing the cooking, one son behind the bar and another son and daughter waiting on the dozen or so tables. The food was traditional *cuisine bourgeoise*, the helpings generous, the good but inexpensive house wine served in earthenware jugs.

'How did you discover this restaurant?' Sophie asked, following Marc's example and mopping up the last of her gravy with a piece of recently baked *pain de campagne*.

'I first came here as a student, when Maman and Papa were in their forties and Célie, their daughter, was still at school. I had a vacation job in our Paris office. For a while I had to live on my wages so I only ate here once a week. My grandfather thought it important to know how the other half live...the people who have to live on a low wage all their lives.'

Earlier, during the first course, he had given her a rundown on the many and various operations under the corporate umbrella, lacing the facts with amusing incidents and insights.

Sophie, who had sometimes found her attention wandering when her ex-boyfriend Robert had talked about his job, had found Marc's exposition riveting. She liked his quirky sense of humour, a trait it was hard to resist in anyone. But she had the feeling she was seeing only one side of him, and that there might be others she would like a lot less.

After dinner they returned to the hotel on foot. As the black calf pumps she was wearing had low heels Marc's suggestion that they should walk didn't dismay her. The exercise and fresh air should help her to sleep on a night when she had many reasons for feeling keyed up.

'One of the things you'll like about living in Venice is the freedom to walk about at night without being molested,' he told her. 'So far, we don't have that problem. I'm not saying there aren't a few areas where it would be unwise to wander with diamonds flashing or a bulging billfold on view. But from being a city where, in centuries gone by, a great many bodies were fished out of the canals with stab wounds and broken skulls it's now as safe and respectable as small-town America was when my grandfather was a young man.'

Although he made frequent references to his grandfather, there was never any mention of his parents, Sophie had noticed. Had something bad happened to them? Was he, like her, an only child? There were so many things she would like to know about him but felt precluded from asking in case he should think her presumptuous.

There was one question she could ask without giving offence.

'Have you ever been to Bordeaux?'

'Only once. Why do you ask?'

'I worked in Bordeaux. It's a beautiful city inside a hell-on-wheels ring road. I had a lovely time there.'

He looked down at her. They were strolling beside the Seine now, and a little chill wind off the river made her glad to be swathed in the soft warmth of her cashmere wrap. Marc appeared not to feel the drop in the temperature. Perhaps it was an effect of his morning run. She had noticed before that men who took a lot of exercise had better circulation than people who didn't.

'I should think you have a lovely time everywhere, don't you, Sophie? You obviously enjoyed your meal tonight, even though that place isn't in any of the good food guides.'

'It deserves to be...but let's hope it stays undiscovered. It might lose its cosy atmosphere if too many foreigners find it. As for having a lovely time everywhere, yes, I guess I do. Isn't that normal for someone my age, with no worries or problems?'

'These days it's unusual to find anyone who makes that claim. Most people seem encumbered by a raft of problems,' he said drily.

'Mmm...I suppose that's true,' she agreed thoughtfully, after a swift mental review of the people she'd known in New York. 'But a lot of people make mountains out of molehills, don't they? Or they don't look at their problems with a clear eye and tackle them.'

Her answer made Marc laugh. 'Where did you learn that attitude? On a self-improvement course? As a matter of interest, one of the islands in the lagoon, Tessera, is used by Edward de Bono, the lateral thinking guru, for courses in self-improvement. That wasn't what brought you to Venice the first time, was it?'

'I've read one of his books but I didn't know about Tessera. Is it near your island?'

'No, it's some way from Capolavoro. You haven't answered my question. Who taught you to look at life with a clear eye? Your parents? One of your teachers?'

She didn't want to tell him who had been the strongest influence on her. Maybe later, when she knew him better.

For the time being it was simpler to say, 'I read a lot. I still do. Most of my ideas come from books.'

'Mine too. What are you reading at the moment?'

'A novel I bought at the airport to read on the plane. But then you turned up so I haven't started it yet.'

'Was it that hard to make up your mind?'

Although she had been careful not to drink too much wine on top of the potent Campari which, in spite of its innocuous colour, was twenty-five per cent alcohol, she was feeling sufficiently laid-back to say frankly, 'Yes, it was…and I'm still not certain I made the right decision.'

'That applies to all life's most challenging commitments,' Marc answered.

As they came to a crossing he put a hand on her shoulder to steer her past the bumpers of cars whose drivers looked set to make competitive starts the instant the lights changed.

She could see that the gesture might have been prompted by the fact that it wouldn't be easy to locate her elbow through the folds of her shawl. But the weight of his hand on the crest of her shoulder, the one farthest from him so that his arm was around her back, although not actually touching it, was a more intimate contact than the conventional hold of a man with patrician manners.

He didn't remove his hand until they had crossed the roadway and walked several yards on. When he did, she realised she had been holding her breath.

By now, ahead, she could see what Americans called the marquee of their hotel: the canopy over the carpet running from the edge of the kerb to the wide steps leading up to a revolving glass door through which passers-by could glimpse the opulence of the flower-decorated lobby.

As they approached the building a taxi drew up and the doorman saluted its passenger, a well-dressed man on his own who bent to hand some notes to the driver.

As he straightened he caught sight of Marc.

'Wash, old buddy... What are you doing in Paris?'

'Hello, Pat. I'm passing through...leaving first thing tomorrow. Sophie, this is Patrick Rivers. We were at school together. Miss Hill has just joined my team. We're on our way to Venice.'

'Delighted to meet you, Sophie.' The other man shook her hand. 'Where did this lucky guy find *you*?'

The emphasis, obviously intended to be flattering, made Sophie's hackles rise. 'In New York,' she said stiffly. 'I was with Masters and Fox.'

He was sure to have heard of them and she hoped to reinforce the fact that she was here on business.

'I bet they're sorry they lost you. I would be,' he said, smiling into her eyes. 'But you're not a New Yorker, are you? That sounds like a British accent.'

Marc answered for her, a tinge of impatience in his voice. 'It is. What are you doing here, Patrick?'

'Stopping by for a drink after a wearing day. Unlike you, I don't have someone like Sophie to soothe my savage breast when head office isn't pleased with the way things are going. What I have is a three-month-old baby who seldom stops bawling and a wife who wishes she hadn't jacked in her career. So do I,' he added, with feeling.

Sophie felt like saying that it might make his wife's life easier if he went home after work instead of stopping by bars. Instead she turned to Marc, 'If you'll excuse me, I'll say goodnight.'

'Goodnight! But the night is young,' Patrick objected. 'You must both come and have a drink with me. I haven't seen Wash in two years. We've a lot of ground to catch up.'

'Not tonight, Pat,' Marc said firmly, following her up the steps.

'Oh, come on, guys, you can't turn in this early... not in Paris,' the other man expostulated.

Then, as Sophie was waiting for someone to emerge from the revolving door before she stepped into it, she heard him add, in French, 'Or maybe you can. Who wouldn't with legs like that pair going up the stairs ahead of him? I'll bet she has splendid boobs too, you lucky...'

By now on her way through the door, Sophie was strongly tempted to turn full circle, give him a box on the ear he wouldn't forget in a hurry and tell him, in the same language, that he was the kind of man who got his sex a bad name.

Resisting the impulse, she marched to the desk for her key and, without glancing over her shoulder, stepped into an open lift and pressed the first-floor button.

CHAPTER FOUR

THE telephone woke Sophie at six-thirty. After thanking the switchboard operator for calling her, she forced herself out of bed and went to take a hot shower.

At seven, a tap on the door heralded the arrival of her breakfast tray. She had ordered fruit, yogurt and herb tea.

At twenty-five minutes past, a baggage porter came for her suitcase. As he disappeared in the direction of the service lift Sophie stepped into a guest lift. In spite of spending the night in the utmost luxury, she couldn't remember when she had last slept so badly.

As she had expected, Marc was already in the lobby, having a friendly chat with the only tailcoated hall porter on duty at that early hour.

'Good morning,' he said as she joined them.

'Good morning.' Her smile was for the porter. 'Good morning.'

'Good morning, *mademoiselle*. I hope you've been comfortable.'

'Very comfortable, thank you.'

'Ah . . . here is your car, Mr Washington. I hope you have a good flight and we shall look forward to your next visit.' The porter ushered them to the door.

Their baggage was already being stowed in the capacious boot as they passed the spot where Marc's schoolfriend had made his offensive remark. Minutes later they were on their way back to the airport.

At first Marc was silent, looking out of the window. Sophie, who had no intention of initiating a conversation, did the same.

It was possible, she realised, that he had forgotten last night's incident. Men looked at life from a different perspective. Even nice men. And she wasn't even sure that, behind the civilised façade, her new employer *was* a nice man.

For all she knew his friend's comments might have amused him. While she went upstairs last night they might have gone to the bar for a drinking session, with Marc assuring the other man that it wouldn't be long before he had added her scalp to the rest of his trophies.

She didn't want to think the worst of him, but why should Patrick have made that obnoxious remark if he didn't know Marc to be a notorious womaniser?

'Werner called me at seven. The weather is clear over the Dolomites so we should have a smooth flight.'

Marc's sudden statement startled her.

'Oh . . . that's good.'

'Have you started your book yet?'

'I read a few pages before I went to sleep.'

She refrained from adding that, in the mood she had been in, the book had failed to grip her. Now she sensed that Marc was looking at her, but she looked at the road ahead. The car had a glass partition between the front and rear seats. The driver couldn't hear his passengers' conversation.

'Patrick didn't know you spoke French. He'd already had a few drinks or he wouldn't have made that remark.'

At that Sophie turned her head to meet the dark eyes focused on her. 'You don't have to make excuses for him. I had already decided I didn't like him before he made it. I imagine it's not at all likely I'll meet him again.' She couldn't resist adding, 'I feel sorry for his wife.'

To her vexation he smiled. 'He's not a bad guy. They're going through a difficult time. The company he works for is in trouble. On top of that the baby's birth wasn't easy and now Alice is exhausted by the baby. It's months since they had sex. Pat is a bundle of frustration, easily turned on by any attractive woman who crosses his path and envious of guys who are single and don't have the worries he has on his shoulders. I feel sorry for them both.'

'He isn't improving the situation by going home late, smelling of Scotch or whatever he drinks.'

'Vodka, which doesn't taint the breath. You're right, of course, but not everyone is as sensible as you are.'

She recognised the hint of irony.

'You think I'm being priggish?'

'Perhaps you have personal reasons for feeling strongly about people who use alcohol as a prop.'

'His drinking is his business. I only object to his rudeness.'

'In fact he was being complimentary... in an unacceptable way,' he added swiftly, forestalling her retort. 'You don't have to spell it out for me. We deal with a lot of accusations of sexual harassment, from the trivial—such as last night's example—to the serious. It's a problem for all employers of mixed-sex staff and our overall policy is to stamp on it—hard. Unless there are extenuating circumstances, as I think there are in Patrick's case.'

While he'd been talking Sophie had come round to the view that perhaps she had taken more umbrage than was justified. She was about to concede this when Marc went on, 'In fact the solution to the problem lies with women themselves. Men learn their fundamental attitudes to women from women... their mothers, their older sisters, their first-grade teachers.'

'Are you suggesting that women are responsible for sexual harassment?'

'You weren't paying attention,' he said, with more than a hint of impatience. 'I was saying that your sex have it in their power to influence masculine behaviour in its formative stages, but often they waste the opportunity and perpetuate inequalities. The mother who expects her daughters to make their beds, keep their rooms in order and help around the house but doesn't demand the same behaviour from her sons is making life difficult for her future daughters-in-law.'

She couldn't disagree with that but was faintly surprised that he understood the burden a domestically incompetent partner could be to a woman with a career. She had met them everywhere she had worked: women struggling to be superwomen because the men they loved were useless—or pretended to be—at coping with and sharing essential everyday chores.

Then, having mollified her, he went on, 'But, on the point you raised, yes, I do feel women bear some responsibility for the way they're treated. Certainly not where violence is involved. There's never any excuse for that. But if they make a habit of wearing tight skirts and revealing tops it shouldn't come as a surprise if someone makes a pass at them at the office party.'

'A lot of passes are made without any justification,' Sophie said shortly. 'The clothes I was wearing last night didn't invite your friend's offensive comments. Even his assumption that I wouldn't understand French was objectionable.'

'If it will make you happier, I gave him a sharp dressing down on your behalf.'

Her startled glance was met with quizzical gleam. The whites of his eyes, she noticed, had the slightly blueish hue of perfect health, and the irises were rimmed by a fine black line almost indistinguishable from their colour except in this bright morning light.

'I should have done it myself,' she said, looking away. 'I don't know why I didn't.'

'Your eyes said everything necessary. He had already got the message before I spelt it out for him.'

A telephone started to ring.

'Excuse me.' He opened a compartment embedded in the centre armrest to answer the call being signalled by a concealed cellphone.

His telephone conversation lasted for some time. It had to do, Sophie gathered, with a contingency being reported from the head office in Germany. Although she was only hearing one side of the conversation, she couldn't help being impressed by his quick grasp of the situation and incisive instructions for handling it.

Whatever else he might be, clearly he was no mere figurehead taking only a cursory interest in the operations which funded his jet-set lifestyle.

By the time he concluded the conversation it seemed wiser not to revive the subject they had been discussing. Probably he had already forgotten it and now had more important matters on his mind.

Most of the interior of Marc's private jet was fitted out as a comfortable sitting room, but it also had a couple of small night cabins, each with its own shower and lavatory. Sophie was shown round by Lisa, a hazel-eyed blonde with the easy friendliness Sophie had found in all the Australians she had met.

After Lisa had served coffee and microwave-heated croissants to Marc, her husband and Leif, the young Swedish co-pilot, on the flight deck, she and Sophie had their croissants together in the main cabin, which was decorated and upholstered in light grey with apricot accents. No commercial airline could compare with this for spacious comfort.

Sophie hoped that Lisa might, without being asked, fill in some of the many gaps in her mental dossier on Marc.

'You're going to love working in Venice now the hot weather's over,' she told Sophie. 'My parents live near the harbour in Sydney and there are moments when Venice reminds me of home. It's the light...the sun on the water. In most other ways they're totally different places, but the light is similar.'

'Your family must miss you,' said Sophie. 'Or do they have other children to help fill the gap?'

'Three...and five grandchildren. We're hoping to go back for Christmas. Werner's mother is dead and his father's remarried. They're not close. He's become part of my family.'

Lisa was forthcoming about her circle, but either she was too discreet to make any reference to her husband's employer or, more likely, she wasn't interested in him except as the source of their income. During the introductions it had been plain to see that she was madly in love with her blue-eyed pilot and that he felt the same way about her.

Sophie envied their happiness and hoped it would last all their lives. Their romance exemplified how much meeting the right person was a matter of luck.

Although her own early life had been shadowed by two examples of horrendously bad luck, she was by nature an optimist, but not to the extent of feeling sure that, out of the millions of wrong men she might encounter, luck would lead her to one of the few who would be an ideal partner. As was proven daily in the divorce courts, the odds were heavily against it.

*　*　*

Her first glimpse of Venice as they approached Marco Polo International Airport, on the edge of the mainland, was profoundly moving.

Fortunately Lisa was also intent on the aerial view of the lagoon. She didn't notice the signs of Sophie's emotion as she peered through the window, her chest heaving, her throat working, her eyes welling with tears as the plane banked and gave her a view of the place where once she had been unforgettably happy.

By the time they touched down on Italian soil she had pulled herself together. The formalities in the airport were brief. Soon her suitcases, and the cases belonging to Lisa and the two pilots, had been put aboard a sleek launch waiting for them at the quay immediately outside the airport. Marc had no luggage. He must have left the clothes he had worn last night and on Concorde in his suite in Paris.

At the stern, behind where Sophie was sitting, a blue and gold pennant fluttered as the launch moved away from the jetty. As they gathered speed she could see that the gold part was a crest, perhaps the insignia of Marc's Venetian forebears.

He was standing beside the stocky man at the wheel while the others relaxed on the side seats, Lisa sitting close to Werner.

Sophie hoped she wouldn't feel another uprush of emotion when the familiar outline of the city appeared on the horizon.

The day she had left Venice, she hadn't, like the other people leaving, had a camera to record her last sight of it. She hadn't needed one. The image had been imprinted on her memory. If she closed her eyes she could see it now. The spreading wash of the boat taking them to the airport. The glittering lagoon, the thick timber piles marking the channels. The beloved skyline, with its many churches and campaniles, gradually disappearing.

'Did you enjoy the flight?'

She opened her eyes to find Marc seating himself beside her, crossing his long legs and raising his arms to rest them on the back of the seat in the same relaxed posture as the pilots.

'Very much, thank you. We had some wonderful views of the Alps, didn't we?'

He nodded. 'I like flying over mountains on a sunny day. But the snow on the Dolomites gives a razor edge to the wind when it blows from that direction.'

'Yes, I remember,' she said.

'You had some cold weather last time?'

It was her turn to nod, hoping he wouldn't ask, wouldn't enquire into the duration of her visit. When the time was right she would explain about 'last time', but this wasn't the appropriate moment.

As Venice came into view Marc said, 'There she is…La Serenissima.'

His caressing tone and the smile at the corners of his mouth struck Sophie as being like of a man who had just seen, in the distance, the woman he loved coming towards him. She wondered if any woman had ever made him look like that, or if his deepest feelings were reserved for what the poet Byron had called a 'fairy city of the heart'.

The walled island, where Venetians were buried, and the city's northern waterfronts were as familiar to her as the streets of West Side New York. She felt her throat tightening again and was thankful she was wearing sunglasses.

Approaching the canal which would take them through the city to the wider and busier waterfront on the south side, the boatman reduced speed. As they cruised slowly past old buildings, the paint on the flaking stucco faded to the hues which made Venice a Mecca for artists, Sophie felt something close to ecstasy. She was back...and suddenly it felt as if she had never been away.

Marc said, 'Your hotel is near the Danieli, but smaller and cosier. A family-run place like the restaurant last night. I thought for the first week or two you would be more comfortable there. Later, if you wish, we can find you an apartment.'

Until he spoke she had assumed she would be housed in the *palazzo*, perhaps in the old servants' quarters. For presumably Venetian *palazzi*, like the stately homes of England, were run differently now from the days when for many people domestic service had been the only option. But perhaps, for a man of Marc's means, finding household staff was as easy as recruiting office staff, and his forebears' palace still had its full quota of minions.

On the jetty where they put in, a youth with a baggage trolley was waiting to take her suitcase from the boatman. Sophie said goodbye to the others and then turned to find that Marc was already on the jetty, waiting to take her hand as she stepped from the swaying launch to the weathered planks of the landing stage.

She had felt the strength in his fingers when they'd shaken hands the day before yesterday, and today his grip was even firmer. The wash of a *vaporetto* arriving at a nearby stop made the launch tilt more forcefully just as she was leaving it.

The water had always been boisterous along this part of the Riva, where there was a lot of traffic coming, going and passing. From lack of recent practice Sophie misjudged the manoeuvre. She sprang up with enough vigour to have made her lose her balance on landing if Marc hadn't hooked a steadying arm round her waist.

For an instant she leaned against him before pulling upright. 'I'm sorry...how clumsy. Thank you.'

'Any time.'

The amused look he slanted down at her gave a nuance to his reply which threw her into confusion. She walked quickly along the jetty in the wake of the youth with the trolley.

The hotel to which he led them had a pavement *caffè* outside it. In the shade of an awning, tourists were writing postcards and drinking coffee and beer.

The lobby was very different from the one in Paris. At present it was piled with the luggage of departing guests, some of whom were standing about waiting to pay their bills. However, when the proprietor saw Marc, he left the desk to shake hands and be introduced.

'Your room is ready for you, *signorina*,' he said, in good English. 'Forgive me for not showing it to you but, as you can see, you have come at a busy time. The boy will take you up and I will talk to you later.'

She looked up at Marc. 'When do you want me to start work? This afternoon?'

'I've been away for some time. I must attend to family matters and you need time to settle in. Spend tomorrow finding your feet and start work the next day,' he said. 'We'll begin by going to Capolavoro. Be on the same jetty at nine.'

Sophie watched him stride from the lobby, the brightness outdoors giving a sheen to his thick dark hair as he stepped into the sunlight and, a few moments later, was gone.

As she followed the baggage porter upstairs she was aware of disappointment that she wouldn't see him again till the day after tomorrow. An absurd reaction when there was nothing she wanted more than to rediscover Venice. A day and a half to explore was a bounty she hadn't expected.

CHAPTER FIVE

TOWARDS the end of the afternoon Sophie was returning to the *albergo* when she caught sight of a man she had known when he was a small boy, with untidy black curls and a mischievous grin.

Now most of his hair was hidden by the red-ribboned straw hat of a gondolier. This was not unexpected. Paolo's father and grandfather had been gondoliers and it was traditional for the skills required to steer the elegant boats around the labyrinth of canals to be handed down from father to son.

What did surprise her was that the skinny boy had grown into a strongly built man, and a handsome one too.

When she first saw him, he was trying to persuade an elderly couple to take a ride in his gondola. After they had shaken their heads and walked on Paolo turned to see if any more prospective customers were among the people coming towards the small hump-backed bridge where he was stationed.

When he spotted Sophie, his first glance was that of a man assessing a woman rather than a gondolier looking for a likely customer. He took in her small waist and her long legs—this afternoon she was wearing dark blue jeans with a checked shirt—and his smile reappeared.

'For you, *signorina*, I make a special price,' he said to her, in English.

However, although he had guessed correctly that she was English-speaking, he obviously had no idea that he was speaking to his first teacher of that language.

'How special?' Sophie asked.

'Very cheap. Only half the official price, because I enjoy showing my city to pretty ladies…especially when they have eyes like the sea in summer,' he added, with a wicked look from his own black eyes.

'You're a poet as well as a gondolier,' she said, smiling, wondering how he would have described her eyes had they been brown or grey. Later, when she had told him who she was, she would ask him.

'I am also a singer,' he told her. 'I have a very good voice. If you come with me, I will sing to you.'

The heads of passers-by turned as he suddenly burst into song, his strong baritone resounding in the narrow street bisected by the canal flowing under the bridge. Translated from the Italian, the words meant, 'Lovely lady, don't break my heart by spurning my devotion.' It sounded like a line from an opera, although Sophie didn't recognise the tune. Or perhaps he had made it up.

'When I sing, everyone listens,' Paolo told her. 'Not like the "serenades" on the Grand Canal.' He put his forefingers in his ears and contorted his face into a grimace of revulsion.

Earlier that afternoon, Sophie had returned to a secluded spot on the Grand Canal, a pleasant corner of the city which non-Venetians found only by accident. There she had perched on a sunny doorstep to watch the water traffic.

Presently three gondolas had come past in line abreast, each packed with as many tourists as they would hold as well as an accordionist and an elderly tenor, their voices long past their best. The music hadn't been quite as ear-splitting as Paolo's mime suggested, but she had to admit it hadn't compared with his short burst of song.

She said, 'I should be embarrassed by the attention you'd attract.'

'Even if I don't sing people will look at us—especially at you. When did you arrive in Venice? Where are you staying?'

'I arrived this morning. I'm staying on the Riva degli Schiavoni.' This wasn't telling him much. There were many hotels on the Riva, catering to every budget level.

'You are not with a group. And if you were here with a lover he would be with you. I think you are here with your parents, who are resting after the journey. If you live in the north of England, a long way from an airport, you had to leave home very early, perhaps before it was daylight.'

'You know a lot about tourists, but you haven't got it right this time. I'm on my own,' said Sophie, wondering if he was married now and chatting up female tourists was merely his stock-in-trade.

Paolo had been leaning against the parapet of the bridge. Now he stood up, 'It's time I took a break. I'll walk you back to the Riva and tell you about some nice places you won't find by yourself.'

'What about your gondola?' she asked, glancing down at the graceful black craft moored alongside the bridge. It was in immaculate order, the sofa upholstered in dark red velvet with matching fringed cushions on the two armchairs facing the stern.

'Nobody is going to steal it. It is not like a speedboat, which any fool can drive if he can start the motor. To steer a gondola is an art. It takes years of practice. Come—I'll show you a short-cut. If you go by the Piazza you will have to push through the crowd on the Ponte della Paglia. Every tourist who comes to Venice wants to photograph the Bridge of Sighs from what you would call the Bridge of Straw. One day it will break under the weight of so many people. At this time of day that bridge is impossible.'

'So I noticed on my way out.' Sophie didn't reveal that she already knew the short-cut he was proposing and had once known Venice as intimately as he did. For a moment she was enjoying the masquerade and looking forward to seeing his astonished stare when she revealed herself. She was also looking forward to asking him about Marc. Paolo would be sure to know something about her employer. The activities of the *palazzo* owners had always been food for gossip in the city.

She wondered how Marc would react if he could see her now, being escorted by a handsome gondolier. It was unlikely they would run into him. If he was out and about this afternoon, it would be in the smart part of Venice, where the banks and the fashionable shops were congregated.

The street they were following was too narrow for more than one person to pass someone coming the other way. Paolo had to walk close behind her until it opened out into one of the many squares called *campi*.

'If not from the north, where are you from?' he asked. 'London?'

'I've worked in London. I like it, but it's choked with traffic. It's pleasanter here, with no cars.'

'All the tourists say that. Listen, if you're alone, why don't you have dinner with me? It's not nice for a girl to have to go to a restaurant on her own in a strange city.'

'That's an old-fashioned idea. Modern women don't mind going about on their own and I'm told Venice is very safe.'

'Yes, but it's more enjoyable to have someone to talk to while you eat your dinner, don't you think?'

'Don't you have a wife to talk to you?'

'I'm not married. I'm still looking.'

Having crossed the *campo* diagonally, they entered an even narrower street which for several yards was roofed like a tunnel by the building spanning it.

'My name is Paolo Sarto. What's yours?' he asked.

She told him without much fear that it would give the game away. Before, he had known her as Kit, a shortened form of a pet name.

'Sophie is nice. It suits you. It sounds gentle and sweet.'

'How come you speak such good English?'

'I speak all the tourists' languages, even some Japanese. It's necessary. I have to tell them about the buildings we pass, about the history of Venice.'

He did not explain his exceptional fluency in her language. Perhaps he had forgotten those early lessons. They were a long time ago.

Outside her hotel, he said he would come for her at a quarter to seven. Sophie didn't demur. She wasn't sure that she would have done even if he had been unknown to her.

She wouldn't have allowed herself to be picked up by a stranger in New York, London or even Bordeaux. But Venice was different. As a group, gondoliers were no less predatory than other men. If they sensed that female tourists were easy conquests, probably some of them made the most of their opportunities. But their ranks were unlikely to include anyone violent. She would have felt safe having dinner with one of them even if she *hadn't* already met his parents, grandparents and numerous aunts and cousins.

Paolo was wearing ordinary clothes when he came for her. Without the straw hat his hair showed thick and curly, but better cut now than when his elder sister, then an apprentice hairdresser, had been his barber.

Sophie had changed her jeans for a short black pleated skirt, opaque black tights and a pale grey cable-patterned sweater with some mohair in it. Although it was hot during the day, after dark the temperature dropped.

'We are going to my aunt's place,' Paolo told her. 'Tourists tell me the food in Venice isn't as good as they find in the rest of Italy, but at Tia Angelita's restaurant you will eat like a princess.'

Sophie remembered his aunt and was certain Tia Angelita would quickly recognise her. Years ago, she had often remarked on the colour of Sophie's eyes.

'You don't remember me, do you, Paolo?' she said as they emerged from an alley into the *campo* dominated by the majestic church of San Zaccaria.

'Remember you?' He looked disconcerted. 'When were you here before? I thought it was your first time.'

She shook her head. 'I didn't think you would ever forget me,' she added, with an exaggerated sigh.

His look of alarm amused her. She could almost hear his brain whirring as he scanned all the girls in his memory for some recollection of her. As he searched wildly for a way to extricate himself from his embarrassing situation she let him squirm for a minute before ending his discomfiture.

'You never used my real name. You used to know me as Kit...short for Kitten. Don't you remember the Englishman who drew caricatures of the tourists? We had a pitch on the Riva. There's a bead stall there now.'

Paolo's forehead wrinkled. 'I remember the old English artist and the girl who looked like a boy... But you can't be her...can you?' He gave her a long searching look. '*Mamma mia!* How you've changed. Who could believe you would grow up to be so beautiful?'

Suddenly seizing hold of her, he gave her the kind of hearty kisses exchanged by close family members after long separations.

Sophie didn't mind being hugged. She liked it. But when Paolo went on to give her a kiss on the lips she pulled back in laughing protest at his quickness to turn the tables and take playful revenge for the trick she had played on him.

'You'll shock the old ladies ... kissing in public,' she said as two smartly dressed elderly women, arm in arm on their evening stroll, came towards them.

'They aren't shocked. They are wishing they were young again,' Paolo said irrepressibly.

And indeed the two stately *signoras* taking their *passeggiata*, a ritual of Venetian life whenever the weather encouraged a leisurely promenade, were looking faintly amused by the young Italian's spontaneous display of affection.

'I still can't believe how beautifully you have grown up,' Paolo said in his own language, when, several hours later, they passed through the same square after a filling meal at his aunt's restaurant and Sophie's reunion with that branch of his family.

His father, Sophie had been sorry to hear, had died two years earlier. His mother was living with a married daughter at Mestre, the industrial town on the shore of the mainland to which many Venetians had moved for jobs in the industries there and for more modern housing.

'You've improved too,' said Sophie. 'But why aren't you married like the others?'

'There's plenty of time. For a man there is never any hurry. Why aren't *you* married?'

'I've been too busy with my career. I'm not here on holiday, Paolo. I shall be working. Have you heard of a man called Marc Washington? His mother was Venetian.'

'Everyone's heard of him. He's one of the richest men in Venice. His father was an American millionaire who fell in love with the daughter of the old Marchese Cassiano. They were all compulsive gamblers, that family. The Palazzo Cassiano was falling to bits due to lack of money to repair it. Then the daughter bewitched this rich Yank and they had one of the grandest weddings this city has ever seen. Mamma's described it to us a thousand times. But a year later she was dead—the bride, I mean. Died in childbirth... And a few years after that her husband drank himself to death.'

'How dreadful.'

It explained why Marc's only family references were to his grandfather, thought Sophie. He hadn't known his parents. She could empathise with that. She hadn't known hers either. But what she did know was that during her parents' few years together they had been deeply happy. The transcript of the tape-recorded log of their last voyage was proof that they had been enjoying life until shortly before the storm which had capsized their boat a few hundred miles from the finish of an ocean race they had been expected to win.

'Why are you interested in Washington?' Paolo asked.

'He's my boss. I'm his personal assistant in Venice, starting the day after tomorrow. He has PAs all over the world—wherever the business empire he inherited operates. I was recruited in New York and met him for the first time the day before yesterday. We flew here together.'

'From what I hear, he's spending big money on one of the islands,' said Paolo. 'Billions of lire, so they say. They're dangerous people, the rich, Kit. You want to watch your step with him.'

She could see it was going to take time for him and his relations to adjust to calling her Sophie. 'What makes you say that? Have you heard bad things about him?'

After a pause, he said, 'Not that I can remember offhand—except that his mother's family were a decadent lot and his father was a dipso. Not genes I'd want in me.'

'We have more than our parents' genes in us. Sometimes people are throwbacks. Marc may take after his grandparents or great-grandparents. Anyway I'm a big girl now. I can look after myself.'

'You don't look as if you can. You don't look as streetwise now as you did when you were a kid. Look, we still have a lot to catch up. If you're not working tomorrow, I'll take the day off as well and we'll spend it together.'

'Can you afford to take days off just like that?'

'Oh, sure. I'm doing well. It helps to be a good-looking fellow with a nice line in sweet talk,' he said, with a mischievous grin.

By now they had reached her hotel. Sophie said, 'It's been an exciting day. I shall sleep like a log. It's been wonderful seeing you all again. Goodnight, Paolo. Thank you for a very happy evening.'

'I'll come for you about ten. That will give you time for a lie-in, if you want one. Goodnight.' He kissed her once, on the cheek, before turning away to walk in the direction of the *piazza*.

An elderly night porter was on duty. He took her room key from a board and reached under the counter for an envelope.

'This was left for you, *signorina*,' he said, in English.

'Thank you. Goodnight.'

As Sophie walked up the staircase she looked at her name on the envelope, written in a boldly incisive hand which could only be Marc's. He must have had it sent round. She wondered why he had written to her when he could have left a telephone message.

In her room, she slit open the plain white envelope and was surprised to find the writing paper inside bore the *albergo's* letterhead. On it was written: 'Change of plan. Report for duty at Palazzo Cassiano at 0900. M.W.'

The extreme terseness of the note, unprefaced by any Dear Sophie and signed only with his initials, made her feel faintly uneasy. But why, since she hadn't been expecting him to call round this evening, should he have been annoyed at finding she had gone out?

Even if she hadn't met Paolo she wouldn't have chosen to eat in the pavement *caffè*, which was the hotel's only restaurant. It did good business by day when the sun was hot, and would be busy on summer nights, but at this time of year after sundown somewhere more sheltered was preferable. If Marc had been displeased at not finding her on the premises he was being rather unreasonable.

On impulse she went downstairs to ask the night porter if he knew when the note had been left.

'It was already here when I came in at half past seven, *signorina*.'

'Thank you. *Buena notte*.'

If she hadn't set her alarm clock Sophie would have overslept. Because her body clock was six hours behind Venetian time, she had fallen into bed with her system still geared to late afternoon in New York—not the right time to be sleeping. She had slept eventually, but not long or soundly enough to feel fresh and clear-eyed at seven.

She got up and opened her window and the dark green shutters which must have been closed by the maid who'd turned down the bed. There was no one about on the Riva to see her in her nightdress, leaning out to adjust the clips which secured the shutters to the wall.

Out in the channel, between the deserted waterfront and the little island of San Giorgio Maggiore, a delivery barge was heading towards the Guidecca, a long strip of land most people outside Venice had heard of only because it had one of the world's most luxurious hotels on it—the Cipriani.

She had a shower and dressed, choosing a straight grey skirt with a generous kickpleat at the back, an ivory silk shirt and her navy blazer. It wasn't part of her job to make fashion statements, but rather to look acceptable wherever her working day might take her. With Marc as her boss that could cover a wide range of venues.

Downstairs, she asked the proprietor, 'How do I get to the Palazzo Cassiano?'

There was a blown-up map of the city on the wall near his desk. He put his finger on the outline representing the palace.

'To walk . . . about twenty minutes—if you don't lose your way,' he said, twinkling at her. 'But we make sure our visitors are never lost for long. Everywhere there are arrows pointing to the Accademia, San Marco and the Rialto. Once you know where those are...no problems.'

Outside, in the *caffè*, Sophie ordered a cheese omelette with toast and tea. By now the Riva was beginning to bustle with groups of students going to their classes. A newsvendor was selling papers to workers on their way to the *vaporetto* stops. A few souvenir-sellers were beginning to set up their stands, although it was too early for there to be organised groups of tourists about.

Her appetite stimulated by the fresh breeze from the lagoon, she would have enjoyed watching all this activity while she ate her breakfast but for an instinctive feeling of uneasiness about Marc's summons.

While drinking a second cup of tea she wrote a note to Paolo, apologising for not being able to spend the day with him.

The *palazzo's* somewhat forbidding street entrance was near the end of a cul-de-sac leading only to the edge of the wide waterway which was the city's principal thoroughfare. There was an old-fashioned iron bell-pull, but also a discreet modern push-button.

Within moments of pressing it Sophie was admitted to the courtyard by an elderly manservant. Even though it was unlikely that in past centuries the family and their equals would have used this entrance, there was an impressive doorway opening into a large hall with a wide staircase.

In the hall, a maid was deputed to show her the way. When they had climbed several flights Sophie understood why the butler had handed her over to someone younger. For ageing joints it would be a strenuous climb to the upper floors of the huge building, with its high ceilings and lavish use of space. Her mind boggled at the thought of the heating bills.

On the top floor she was shown into a large empty room. With a shy smile the maid went away. Sophie was drawn to the windows with their wide views over the city's Roman-tiled rooftops and distinctive flowerpot-shaped chimneys.

As the great bell of San Marco began to strike nine, backed by a chorus of chimes from near and far bell-towers, she sensed rather than heard Marc enter the room behind her.

'Good morning.' His tone was curt, his expression unsmiling. He was wearing freshly laundered jeans and an open-necked pale blue shirt with a navy sweater slung round his shoulders, the sleeves loosely tied on his chest. 'I hope you found your accommodation satisfactory.'

'Extremely comfortable, thank you, and the view from my window is superb.'

'Good.' He moved to an outsize desk, seating himself behind it and indicating that she should take the chair in front of it.

The desk had a sheet of glass protecting the patina of its antique mahogany surface. On one side stood a small-footprint PC, on the other a tray containing such things as a letter-opener, long-bladed scissors, pens and markers. There were no photographs, and none of the costly accessories found on most VIPs' desks.

'Did he make a pass at you?'

The blunt question rattled her. How did he know she had spent the evening with a man?

When she didn't answer immediately, he said, 'That's the usual form with susceptible tourists. I thought you had more sense than to fall for a gondolier's line of flattery.'

Sophie began to recover herself. 'Did you see us together? How did you know he was a gondolier?'

'No, I didn't see you. The owner of your hotel recognised him. There aren't many *gondolieri* left. They're a diminishing species, most of them known by sight if not by name to the older inhabitants. The one who picked you up is one of the youngest... and a well-known Casanova.'

His assumption that it must have been a pick-up made Sophie angry. For Paolo it had been that. Not for her. But if Marc was ready to jump to derogatory conclusions about her, let him.

CHAPTER SIX

SOPHIE said coldly, 'Hearsay isn't always reliable. Hardly ever, in my experience. He behaved with the utmost courtesy. We ate at a restaurant run by his aunt and uncle where the food was very much better than I might have eaten elsewhere.'

'And where he wouldn't have to pay,' Marc said drily. 'Are you seeing him again?'

'I expect so.' Common sense dictated that she explain the situation, but offended pride and resentment at his unjust assumption made her leave it at that, apart from adding, 'I'd like to master the Venetian dialect while I'm here. A gondolier and his family are useful contacts.'

His tilted eyebrow was sceptical. 'You can do as you please in your free time. But don't be surprised if there turns out to be some truth in what you dismiss as hearsay.'

Still annoyed with him, but beginning to realise that the situation had lent itself to misinterpretation, Sophie said, 'I'm sorry I wasn't there if you needed me to work on something last night. If you'd telephoned, instead of coming to the hotel, you might have caught me before I went out.'

'I came to take you out myself.'

Disconcerted, she said, 'Oh ... well, that was kind of you.'

Almost echoing Paolo, he said, 'I thought you might be uncomfortable eating alone at night. Some women are.' He rose from his chair. 'Before we go over to

Capolavoro I'll show you where it is in relation to the other islands in the lagoon.

'This shows the whole lagoon,' he said moments later, when she was standing beside him in front of the large wall map.

It was as familiar to her as the layout of Manhattan Island or central London. She was watching his hand, not the map, as he said, 'All the islands in the lagoon were important once. They were only accessible by boat and each had its special function. Then Venice was linked to the mainland by railway bridge and a canal was dredged from the city to the Lido. After that the other islands weren't important any longer and gradually most were abandoned.'

Sophie was listening to what he was saying, but her visual attention was on the strong, sunburned hand pointing out the features he was telling her about.

Suddenly she found herself wondering how many women had felt those long fingers on their skin, and if he had given them pleasure as well as taking it.

Faintly embarrassed by the inappropriateness of this unbidden thought, she was slow in reacting when he said, 'And the other map shows the *valli*—the traditional fish farms.'

If her thoughts hadn't been wandering, she would have anticipated his movement towards the other map. They would have both moved sideways at the same time. As it was, her delayed response caused him to bump into her.

Although it was her fault, it was he who said, 'I'm sorry.'

Startled by the effect of the contact between his chest and her shoulder and upper arm, she said nothing. Such light, unimportant impacts were frequent on the New York subway or the London Underground at rush hour.

People might murmur 'Sorry' or they might ignore them. They certainly didn't react the way she was reacting now.

As he started explaining the locks and sluices controlling the fish ponds she felt a lingering vibration deep inside her, as if her nerves were harp-strings he had plucked and left quivering.

It was a relief when he finished his explanation. It was not that she wasn't interested in the ancient and intricate system of fish farming in the lagoon. But it was hard to concentrate when he was standing as close as he was at the moment.

Perhaps this strange over-sensitivity was an after-effect of changing time zones. He did it all the time and his system was used to it. Hers wasn't.

As they went down the stairs it struck her that she hadn't felt normal from the moment he'd entered her life. There was something intensely disturbing about him. She had never seen a tiger in reality. But sometimes, on TV, powerful zoom lenses allowed close-up shots in which the great beasts seemed to be looking directly into the eyes of the viewer.

There was a connection between the way she had felt when Marc had been looming over her, his sleeve almost brushing hers, and her response to tigers. With their beautiful markings, the formidable power concealed by the dense velvet fur and their strange, enigmatic eyes, they exuded animal magnetism. They could also be deadly dangerous, especially those who were man-eaters.

Instinct warned her that Marc had a lot in common with tigers and might be an incorrigible woman-eater.

They left the *palazzo* by the main entrance. The launch which had fetched them from the airport was waiting, with the same boatman.

'These are called *pali*,' said Marc, indicating the tall posts, painted with spiralling strips, projecting from the

water on either side of the well-kept, moss-free steps.
'The colours are like the silks worn by jockeys. They tell
anyone interested in such things to whom each *palazzo*
belongs . . . or belonged originally.'

Marc had just followed her inboard when a *vaporetto*
came by, some of its passengers looking with curiosity
at the two people in the launch moving away from the
steps of the magnificent palace.

Although it was already hot in the sun, Sophie knew
there would be a cool breeze when they reached open
water. She didn't take off her blazer. For seeing the island
jeans would have been more appropriate. She would have
to ask Marc how he felt about her wearing trousers on
duty.

Last night it had seemed lucky to run into Paolo on
her first day in Venice. Now she wished it hadn't happened yet. She didn't want to lose Marc's good opinion
of her, but nor did she want to explain her past to him.
Not until after she had been back to *her* island.

On the way to the island that Marc had leased he told
her it had the remains of a fortress on it and the ruins
of several small houses built by people who must have
lived on what they could grow and fish from the surrounding lagoon.

He unrolled a plan he had brought with him. It showed
the shape of the island and the site for the house he
planned, with architect's visualisations of how it would
relate to the fort, which his lease obliged him to restore.

They spent about an hour on Capolavoro. Long before
they left she had grasped how important the project was
to him. To anyone else the place would look a desolate
spot with nothing appealing about it. But, if he could
realise his vision of it, in a few years' time it would look
very different.

It was nearly noon when they returned to the *palazzo*. Marc said, 'I'll show you your office. It has the basic equipment common to all the other PAs' offices, but you're free to order anything you consider necessary from the shops where I have accounts. You'll find a list of them on my PC. This week's password is Constanzia. I rotate the names of my three aunts.'

Her office was across the landing from his large room. It was small but, to her delight, it had a glass door leading onto a little roof garden with tubs of greenery and a table and chair with a furled parasol standing beside it.

'If you like, while the hot weather lasts, you can have your lunch here. Alternatively, there's a large garden at street level. You're welcome to take your coffee and lunch breaks down there. But my aunts spend a good deal of time in the garden and they're all extremely talkative. You could find them tiring. I do,' he added drily.

As he finished speaking a young female voice called in Italian, 'Marc...Marc...where are you?'

He returned to the doorway. 'I'm here. Come and meet my new assistant.'

It was difficult to guess the age of the girl who appeared seconds later, giving him a radiant smile. Her lovely skin was that of someone very young, but Sophie had never seen anyone of eighteen or nineteen who was so perfectly groomed or self-possessed.

She was wearing a very short geranium-red tunic, cinched at the waist by a wide leather belt, with tights, shoes and lipstick of the same colour and huge silver earrings and bracelets. She might have stepped straight from the cover of Italian *Vogue*.

'I've been looking everywhere for you,' she said, laying a long-fingered hand with geranium-lacquered nails on his forearm.

Marc said, 'Sophie, this is my cousin Chiara Banti...Sophie Hill.'

'Welcome to Venice, Ms Hill,' the Italian girl said warmly, offering her hand.

She spoke American English with only the faintest trace of an Italian accent, and was clearly *au fait* with modern forms of address.

'Thank you,' Sophie said admiringly. She had never seen a lovelier girl.

Barefoot, their heights would be similar. But Sophie was wearing flat-heeled tassel loafers and Chiara was perched on absurdly high heels attached to her feet by a few narrow straps. They were obviously very fashionable, but for wearing in an old house and a city of numerous bridges they seemed strikingly impractical.

'What did you want me for?' asked Marc.

'I can't decide what to wear for the party tonight. I want you to help me choose.'

'Later. Right now we're busy. Ask me again after lunch.'

She looked disappointed. 'Oh...all right.' With another smile for Sophie she left.

Marc led the way back to his room. There, with the girl out of earshot, he said, 'Don't let Chiara make a nuisance of herself. She's bored, having nothing to do but go to parties and amuse herself. She ought to be starting a career but she has a very silly, possessive mother who never trained for anything and sees no reason why Chiara should. I'm working on her to change her mind but Tia Caterina is a recent widow. Although she and her husband were often at odds while he was alive, she's behaving as if the sky had fallen in.'

'Perhaps it has,' said Sophie. 'Couples don't have to be blissfully happy to feel bereft when one of them dies. How old is Chiara?'

'Twenty-two, but she behaves more like sixteen. She's been impossibly spoilt but has somehow managed to survive it and become a very sweet girl. You'll have to be firm with her, though. Given the smallest encouragement, she'll come up here and chatter for hours.'

For the next hour or so he gave her a thorough briefing on what was expected of her. Then he departed to lunch with his family.

'You'll meet the rest of them later. Rather than sitting through a long formal luncheon downstairs, I am sure you'd rather have a light lunch up here and get on with the process of settling in. I'll be out this afternoon, but I'll look in about four-thirty to see how you're getting on.'

After he had gone, Sophie wondered if the truth was that his aristocratic relations would not find a foreign employee an acceptable presence at their table. But he was right: she was happier eating up here.

At that moment the house telephone started ringing. When Sophie had answered it, *'Pronto, sono Sophie,'* a man's voice replied that he was the chef, and what would the *signorina* like to eat today? She had only to state her wishes and they would be fulfilled.

At the end of a delicious lunch starting with asparagus mousse followed by trout with almonds and stuffed courgettes, Sophie's final treat was a generous slice of *zuccotto* — a cake made of sponge, ice cream, chocolate and cream.

I can't eat like this every day, she thought, enjoying the last mouthful. Perhaps it's the three aunts who polish off most of the fattening dishes. Marc and Chiara don't. It would take more than a morning run to keep him lean if *he* ate like this every day.

She had been offered wine with her meal but had asked for spring water and *camomilla* instead of coffee. Italian coffee was strong and she didn't want to drink a lot of it.

After brushing her teeth in the washroom that Marc had said was for her use only, she checked all the stationery and equipment in her office. There were several things she would need in order to work in the way she found most efficient. After making a note of them, she went to his room to check the list of shops he had mentioned.

Sophie had once read that a man's office was an indication of his character as well as his position. Here were none of the usual status symbols: the paintings by recognisably important artists, the photographs of encounters with statesmen and royalty, the antique humidor or the silver box for cigars, the trifles from Tiffany or Cartier. The most striking features of *this* room, after its views, were the wall of books and the wall of pictures and posters, even including some postcards which had obviously caught its occupant's eye.

Both walls confirmed that he was a man whose life was spent travelling, sometimes to parts of the world which had nothing to do with his commercial empire. There were books about primitive people living in remote places, and paintings by unknown artists. As she scanned the pictures her eye was arrested by one only recognisable for what it was by someone who knew every inch of this city.

It was a pen-and-wash drawing of a Venetian cat sleeping curled in the metal folds of the skirt belonging to a female figure at the base of an equestrian statue of an Italian king on the Riva near her hotel. But not many people would recognise the border on the sculpted skirt unless, like herself, they had spent long hours near that spot.

She wondered what had prompted Marc to buy that particular piece of art. Did he like cats? Or was it the contrast between the cat's soft fur and the burnished metal which had appealed to him? Later, she would ask.

The computer on his desk was, she knew, for his private use, and not linked to the one on her desk or accessible to anyone without permission. She was a little surprised he should allow her to use it.

Sophie was familiar with most of the applications in widespread use, and as Marc had written down the path to the list she needed she had no difficulty in finding it and printing a copy.

She couldn't resist finding out how well organised he was on his computer. All the other areas of his life were serviced by people like his butler, his boatman, his chef and a worldwide retinue of paid retainers who, if they weren't efficient, were replaced by people who were. But how successful would he have been if he hadn't been born into money?

It was the work of a moment to find out that he had a very large number of items stored on disk. After ten minutes' browsing, she was impressed by the way he had them organised. It was possible someone else had tailored the arrangements for him, but she didn't think so. It had all the hallmarks of a customised set-up, devised and used by a man with a brilliant mind in total command of the technology he was using.

During the afternoon various telephone calls and faxes required her attention, including a note from Audrey LaRue wishing her well in her new job.

At four o'clock, while she was typing a letter to Merle, she heard Marc's footsteps on the staircase. When he had looked at the messages and given her some instructions for dealing with them, he said, 'But all that can wait till tomorrow. First, I'll show you some more of the house...the rooms that are only used on special occasions.'

The larger staterooms were awesome in their splendour, with chandeliers, huge paintings and ornate gilded furniture. The only room having any claim to comfort was a bedroom with papered walls and a curtained bed with some pretty porcelain displayed in the alcoves on either side of it.

'This is where, by tradition, the brides of my mother's ancestors had their first experience of the pleasures, or otherwise, of the marriage bed,' said Marc.

He turned to the wall that the bed faced. 'There's a curious story attached to this looking-glass. As you see, it's a much finer example than the one you feel has been vandalised in our New York office.' There was a hint of mockery in the glance he turned on her. 'This one has hung here for several centuries—except for one short period when it was moved to another room in which an important guest was to sleep for a few nights. During the first night she had a peculiar experience.'

He turned away to admire the artistry of the reflective glass frame surrounding the time-misted centre panel. Sophie, impatient for him to go on, watched the reflection of his face. When their eyes met in the mirror she found she couldn't look away.

'What happened?' she asked.

'The visitor didn't sleep well. She was sitting up in bed by the light of a candle when something strange happened. She was the unmarried daughter of a middle-European king who had lost his throne, and her lady-in-waiting was sleeping in the next room. The princess insisted she came and slept with her.'

'Do you mean she'd seen something frightening in the mirror?' Sophie asked.

'It frightened her. It wouldn't have frightened me. I don't know how you would have reacted.'

She suspected him of prevaricating to tease her. Perhaps the whole story was a tease.

'What *did* she see?'

'They both saw it. They left the candle alight and eventually the princess slept while the lady-in-waiting read. According to written reports of what happened— in the notes and letters people wrote before they could gossip by telephone—she was a level-headed young woman. Rather like you, probably.' Again the dark eyes reflected in the misty glass held a glimmer of mockery.

'I should have blown out the candle and gone to sleep,' said Sophie.

'Perhaps the princess snored or the book was interesting. At any rate, some time later she glanced at the mirror and saw and heard much the same as the princess had seen and heard . . . two people making love, in a different bed, in a different room. This room.'

'I think you're inventing this. To me it sounds pure tarradiddle,' Sophie said, using a word from her childhood.

'I promise you I'm not. Ask Chiara—ask my aunts when you meet them. Half Venice knows the story of the Palazzo Cassiano's haunted mirror.'

Not wholly convinced, she said, 'If such a thing really did happen, or they claimed it did, the princess and her attendant were either dreaming or hallucinating. It sounds about as believable as that story of the two women who claimed to have seen Queen Marie Antoinette when they were visiting Versailles.'

A thought struck her. 'I'm sure *you* don't believe it. If you did, when you were younger you'd have spent the night here to see for yourself.'

'When I was fourteen I did, and very scary it was— far away from the rest of the household in the small hours. Various people have tested the legend, including my mother when she was young. She had a group of friends to keep her company.'

'But none of you saw what the princess thought she had seen?'

'Disappointingly, no. But the legend persists.'

'As ghosts stories go, it's rather a nice one,' said Sophie.

'Actually, no,' he said drily. 'What the lady-in-waiting saw was different from what the princess saw. She, being an elderly spinster, was shocked by the erotic nature of her vision. Nowadays my aunts watch similar scenes on TV and think nothing of it. But this was in 1843 and—'

He was interrupted by a bleeping from his shirt pocket.

'Excuse me... somebody wants me. There's a house phone in the corridor. Which reminds me,' he added, leading the way, 'I must give you a bleeper. In a house this size it's as essential as a watch.'

Sophie followed him back the way they had come and stood at a polite distance while he checked with whoever had bleeped him.

Then, to her amazement, he put his hand over the mouthpiece and said, 'It's Domenico, our major-domo, with a message for you. There's a gondolier at the street door, asking what time you stop work. I gather you've set up another date with him tonight?'

CHAPTER SEVEN

'NOT to my knowledge.'

Sophie couldn't believe that Paolo could have made such a maladroit move as to call for her on her first day at the *palazzo*. She felt furious with him.

'It wasn't a "date" last night,' she added crisply. 'Please ask Domenico to tell him I can't come down now and not to wait for me.'

But what Marc said to his butler was, 'The *signorina* will be down in five minutes. We're on the first floor and she has to fetch her purse from the office.' Then he replaced the receiver. 'It's knocking-off time anyway. He may have come to take you back in his gondola. You must introduce us. I'm curious to meet this guy.'

Inwardly Sophie was fuming. But there was nothing she could do but accept the situation and make sure Paolo never repeated his *faux pas*.

She debated explaining to Marc about knowing Paolo years ago, but she knew this wasn't the right moment. Not while they were hurrying up a staircase he climbed two steps at a time while she had to run to keep pace with him.

She was breathless when they reached the top floor, and it didn't mollify her when Marc said casually, 'New York has made you decadent. By the time you've been here a month, you'll whizz up and down our stairs and think nothing of it.'

Trying not to pant and determined not to be nettled, at least not visibly, she said pleasantly, 'I'm sure I shall.

They're good exercise—which I'll need if lunch always ends with a pudding as rich as today's *zuccotto*.'

'It's not generally realised that the French learnt the art of cooking from the Italians,' said Marc. 'It was Catherine de' Medici's cooks, who took their arts to France when she married the French king Henri II, who gave French cuisine its impetus.'

'I've met Frenchmen who don't agree with that theory,' said Sophie, picking up her shoulder-bag.

'Do you want to touch up your lipstick before we go down?'

She suspected him of deliberately trying to exacerbate her embarrassment.

'No, thanks,' she said composedly.

Paolo, wearing his gondolier's clothes, was waiting for her in the courtyard inside the street door. Domenico was with him, but he went away when he saw his employer and Sophie descending the stairs from the first door.

Paolo's straw hat was on the stone table near where he was standing. 'I got your note,' he told Sophie as she came down the last steps. Then his gaze shifted to Marc.

Before she could introduce them, Marc introduced himself, by name and as her employer. At the same time he offered his hand. There was no condescension in his tone. His manner was as friendly as if socially they were equals.

In fact they were not unalike. They could have been half-brothers, Marc the son of an aristocratic marriage and Paolo born outside marriage to a girl from one of the city's poorest quarters. Their heights were different, and their features, but both looked unmistakably Venetian. Faces like theirs could be seen in paintings of La Serenissima's citizens from the centuries when it had been the gateway between Europe and the riches of the East.

'I hope I'm not interrupting anything, but I thought . . . er . . . Sophie might like to ride back with me. The *vaporetti* are crowded at this time of day,' said Paolo. She guessed it had been on the tip of his tongue to call her Kit.

'I intended to walk,' she said. 'It's not far.'

Marc said, 'I would have walked with you and shown you the stationery shop where we buy our supplies. But I expect you can find it by yourself. Enjoy your ride in a gondola. If you weren't an attractive blonde you would have to pay through the nose for it.'

For a moment he seemed about to turn away and go through the door at the foot of the stairs. Instead he gestured for her to go first through the street door and followed her.

Being called an attractive blonde made Sophie bristle. Although, on her holidays with Merle, days in the sun had bleached her hair to a much lighter shade than her present degree of fairness, she didn't think of herself as a blonde, and certainly not in the pejorative sense of being the dizzy or dumb blonde implied by his tone.

She was feeling annoyed with both of them when they reached the end of the street where the gondola was moored.

Paolo sprang lightly into the well. 'I'd better lift you down. Put your hands on my shoulders.'

As he spoke Marc took hold of her bag's strap. 'I'll take this and pass it to you.'

'Thank you.'

It wasn't the first time a gondolier had put his hands on her waist and lifted her into his craft. Paolo's father had done it. She remembered his florid face, his nicotine-stained teeth and the smell of tobacco and wine on his breath.

Paolo's face was the colour of teak, his teeth were white and he smelt of the clove-scented toothpaste called

Pasta del Capitano they had used when she was a child. The faint whiff of it brought back those years with the poignancy of a grief which had never quite healed.

The Italian set her on her feet, taking hold of her hand until she was seated on the sofa. Then he took her bag from Marc, dropped it lightly on her lap and stepped past her to his place on the stern.

Marc gave them a farewell wave, his expression sardonic. She hoped he would walk away but he stayed where he was. Using his single oar, Paolo propelled them in the direction of the Santa Maria della Salute, the church like a giant wedding cake at the eastern end of the Grand Canal, and she did not look over her shoulder to see if Marc was still there.

She was thinking that if it hadn't been for the man behind her she could have been walking through the city with the other one, perhaps stopping for a drink in a street *caffè* and hearing the rest of the story he had been telling her.

Apart from agreeing that it was a beautiful evening, Sophie was a silent passenger—at first because she was angry and then because the soothing motion of the gondola and the beauty of the scene before her combined to calm her annoyance. It reminded her that where she was and what she was doing was something people trapped in the world's many ugly cities would consider a taste of paradise.

By the time the canal had widened into the glittering expanse of the *bacino* and the long line of elegant buildings along the Riva were beginning to be tinted with the rose glow of evening, her irritation had subsided.

Very near her hotel there were unadorned wooden stakes, poor relations of the painted *pali* outside the *palazzi*, driven into the bed of the lagoon as moorings for gondolas. Instead of steering towards them, Paolo kept the bow pointing parallel with the Riva.

'Where are we going?' said Sophie, turning to look at him.

From his place on one side of the stern he smiled down at her. 'I'm taking you for a drink . . . but not at the clip-joint prices the tourists pay.'

For a moment she thought of insisting that he drop her off on the Riva, but decided it would be better to remonstrate when he didn't have part of his mind on the water traffic.

Although it bore no relation to the rush-hour traffic snarls in New York or London, at this time of day the *bacino* was criss-crossed by the white wakes of engine-driven craft. Gondoliers had to be more watchful now than in the days when Paolo's grandfather had been plying his trade.

The broad esplanade of the Riva was cut into sections by canals crossed by small hump-backed bridges. As they glided beneath one some tourists leaning on the parapet took snaps of the good-looking gondolier. Without turning round, Sophie felt sure he was flashing his white teeth at them. He had always played to the gallery, she remembered, but not in an unpleasant way. The grown-ups had told him off, but pinched his cheek or patted his head as they did it.

In the smaller canals it was quiet, except when they came to a blind bend and Paolo's warning *'Ohé!'* would ring out.

Where two canals crossed, they gave way to another gondola carrying two portly couples.

'You can't be short of a bob, love,' one of the men called to Sophie in a broad northern accent. 'We're going to be skint after this lot. They know 'ow to charge in this town.'

Sophie smiled but said nothing, wondering if Paolo would understand what skint meant.

Evidently the other gondolier had understood his passenger's last remark. In the Venetian dialect, he said to Paolo, 'They all complain about prices. They have no values, these people. To ride through Venice in a gondola is a once-in-a-lifetime experience. When my sons are men it may no longer be possible. These stupid people should be grateful they can afford to come here. Do they think we want millions of them invading our unique city?' He looked at Sophie, his expression softening. 'She's pretty. You always get the pretty ones. I get the fat, ugly ones.'

'Would you rather work on an assembly line in a factory in Mestre?' Paolo asked him as the other gondola was disappearing from view.

'The prices here are rather steep,' Sophie remarked.

'We have to cover the months when we don't make any money. It's a vicious circle,' said Paolo. 'Without the tourists the city would fall into ruins, but now there are too many of them. In the old days they stayed longer and enjoyed themselves more. At this season it's not so bad, but in the summer... a madhouse!'

But the square where he stopped the gondola was an oasis of peace, with only a few local people enjoying the last of the sunlight at the tables outside a *caffè*.

When he had ordered their drinks, he said, 'Why did you have to work today? I thought you weren't starting till tomorrow?'

'My boss changed his mind. Paolo, you shouldn't have come to the *palazzo*. I don't have fixed working hours like other people. A PA's hours are elastic.'

'You didn't tell me your boss was a young man. I haven't seen him before. I thought he was much older. Didn't you want him to know you have a boyfriend?' he said shrewdly.

'You're a friend, not a boyfriend,' she said firmly.

'Have you grown so grand since you left us that a gondolier isn't good enough for you any more?'

'Your job has nothing to do with it. We were close as children, but now we're two grown-up people who don't really know each other. I've changed and I'm sure you have. Life is more complicated now than it was all those years ago.'

'For you, perhaps. Not for me. What are you looking for, Kit?'

'I'm Sophie now,' she reminded him. 'At the moment I'm not looking for anything. Having just landed an exceptional job, I have to concentrate on doing it well. Marc Washington is a very demanding employer. If I don't come up to scratch, he'll replace me.'

Their drinks came: a beer for him, *spritz al bitter* for her. It tasted subtly different from the one in Paris. Perhaps it was like some wines which, in wine buffs' jargon, 'didn't travel'. Maybe Campari never tasted the same outside Italy, and never quite as perfect as in the roseate twilight at the close of a day in Venice.

'Tonight we won't eat at Tia Angelita's place,' said Paolo. 'I want to have you to myself. I want to find out how you've changed . . . if you've really changed.'

Presently he rowed her through the twists and turns of the smaller waterways back to the Grand Canal, to a restaurant where the canal-side tables were full of well-heeled tourists. He had reserved a table by one of the windows in an upstairs room. Here the patrons were mainly Venetians eating their *antipasti*, mostly dishes of seafood. Sophie recognised *moleche*, the crabs caught in spring and autumn when they changed their shells.

Having eaten well at lunchtime, she wasn't very hungry and could only manage a bowl of fish soup and a salad. Paolo ate four courses and finished with cheese. Although he was trim and muscular at the moment, she thought that if he didn't take care he would run to fat later.

At the end of their meal, while they were drinking coffee—his accompanied by a glass of *grappa*—Sophie glanced out of the window and saw a launch flying a blue pennant cruising slowly along the canal in the direction of the Rialto Bridge.

Seated in the stern, wearing a dinner jacket, was Marc. Beside him, in a fur jacket with a rug over her legs, was his young cousin Chiara.

Something in Sophie's expression made Paolo turn his head to see what she was looking at. 'That's your boss, isn't it? Who's the chick with him?'

'A cousin...Chiara Banti. I met her today. She said she was going to a party but I didn't know he was going with her.'

'Jealous?' said Paolo, taking his eyes off the launch passing below them long enough to flash a grin at her.

'Don't be silly.' Sophie tried to speak lightly, not to betray how much his quip annoyed her. 'There's nothing I'd enjoy less than going to a fashionable party where I wouldn't know anyone.'

'If you were with him it wouldn't matter. He knows everyone. When you have his money and his background, everyone wants to know you. If there was any justice in life, he'd have a face like an ape,' said Paolo. 'She's a good-looker too, but too young for my taste. They still giggle a lot at that age and they want to dance all night. I'm past that.' He stopped watching the launch and turned to her. 'Quiet, candlelit dinners with someone intelligent are what I prefer these days.'

Next morning, very early, Sophie went for a brisk walk along the Riva. In New York she and Merle had attended exercise classes, but here she thought she might buy some trainers and take up running.

She wondered where Marc did his running when he was in Venice. She didn't expect to meet him. It was more likely he ran along the Zattere, the waterfront on the south side of the élite Dorsoduro district, not far from his *palazzo*. But if he and Chiara had been partying half the night he might postpone today's run until later.

Paolo's chaffing remark about jealousy still rankled slightly. Paolo himself was a complication in her life. It wasn't true, as he had suggested last night, that the company of a gondolier and his family wasn't good enough for her now. It was merely that she didn't want Marc to think she had been bowled over by Paolo, like the susceptible tourists who every year lost their hearts to Italian and Spanish waiters, Greek boatmen, Swiss and Austrian ski-instructors and all the other good-looking young men who worked in the tourist industry and notched up innumerable conquests which meant nothing to them.

Yesterday, if Paolo hadn't turned up and Marc had walked her back to the Riva, she would have explained the situation to him. But it was quite a long story and needed to be told in the right circumstances, not when he had more important matters on his mind.

On the way back from her walk she stopped in the Via Giuseppe Garibaldi, a filled-in canal which was now the city's widest street but far enough from the Piazza to have a village atmosphere and for the prices in the bars and *alimentari* to be much cheaper. Sophie bought two brown rolls for breakfast and a bag of apples for her room. She ate the rolls as they were, sitting on a stone bench with the kind of view which had inspired Canaletto to paint his stupendous vistas of eighteenth-century Venice.

All the happiness she had once known in this city was beginning to seep through her veins like the rising sap in a tree. Love was no longer here: the shared laughter, the physical comfort of a strong shoulder to lean on and the warm hugs and bristly kisses. But Michael's spirit was here. She felt his presence everywhere, and heard in her mind his deep voice calling her Kitten, Sweetie and other endearments.

She arrived at the *palazzo* at a quarter to nine, reaching the top floor to find Marc already there.

'Good morning,' she said, from the threshold of his office.

'Good morning.' He rose from behind the wide desk. 'A lot has come through overnight.' He indicated the tray behind the fax machine. 'I've dealt with some of it already. We'll go through the rest together and I'll tell you what needs to be done.'

'I'll just fetch my notebook.'

In her office, Sophie hung her blazer on the hanger in the cupboard.

Freshly shaven, his dark hair still damp from the shower, Marc looked alert and well-rested. Perhaps he didn't need much sleep. It was a peculiarity of many top-level achievers that they could maintain their physical and mental energy on half the sleep required by the average person.

'Did you enjoy your evening?' she asked, when she rejoined him. 'I saw you and Signorina Banti going past in the launch while I was having supper.'

'Chiara enjoyed herself. I was there as her chaperon. Large parties are not my personal choice for a night out. I prefer a quiet dinner *à deux*. Where did you eat?'

When she told him, he raised an eyebrow. 'Alone?'

She wished now she hadn't mentioned seeing him. 'No.'

'That restaurant's expensive,' said Marc. 'Your gondolier must be seriously enamoured. Are you seeing him again tonight?'

'No, I'm not...and it isn't—'

But Sophie's decision to explain her relationship with Paolo was frustrated by the telephone.

'Excuse me.' He reached for the receiver. *'Pronto, sono Washington.'* A moment later he was speaking Japanese and signing to her that the call would take some time.

Later she accompanied him to a meeting with his architect and representatives of the city's planning authority.

They walked to the architect's office where he was going to show them a scale model of Capolavoro's existing and proposed buildings.

On the way there many people said good morning to Marc, but not always, Sophie noticed, the kind of people who might be expected to know him. Two or three of his acquaintances were noticeably down-at-heel. Even more surprising was what happened as they mounted the wooden steps of the Accademia Bridge, where a man was crouched, begging.

There were not many beggars in Venice. So far Sophie had seen only two, and on each occasion had responded with a small donation. But most people, especially tourists, ignored them and she wouldn't have been surprised if Marc had done the same. Instead, they both put their hands in their pockets and gave the man some money.

At the top of the bridge Marc stopped, putting his palms on the edge of the sun-warmed balustrade and looking down the broad waterway with the same slightly smiling expression she had seen when they'd been approaching the city from the airport.

Standing beside him, watching a gondola going in the direction of the Rialto and a delivery barge chugging in the opposite way, she said, 'Do you always give to beggars...even when they're probably dipsos?'

Marc turned his head to look at her. 'If they've hit the rock-bottom point of asking strangers for money, the least I can do is give them the price of a drink. It's an ineffective way of addressing the problem of these people who can't cope with life, but it's better than pretending not to notice them. I thought you would be a soft touch.'

'Did you? Why?'

A light gust of breeze off the water caught and ruffled her hair, blowing a lock of it across her cheek. Before she could deal with it he reached out and did it for her, smoothing the errant strands behind her ear. The intimate, almost tender gesture astonished her.

He began to walk on. 'You strike me as someone who would always be on the side of the underdog,' he said. Then, slanting a mocking glance at her, he added, 'But perhaps not always equally sympathetic to the problems of the top dogs. Except in your professional capacity.'

After the meeting, Marc and the architect went off to have lunch together while she returned to the *palazzo* to transcribe her record of what had been said.

Although she had contributed little to the men's conversation, but had sat quietly by, taking verbatim notes while they talked, from the outset Marc had made it clear that when he was away she would be left in full charge of the island's conversion.

Whether she really had his confidence to the extent he had indicated she herself wasn't sure. But he had left the others in no doubt of it. The architect had pressed her to join them for lunch but she had thought it best to excuse herself.

A printout was on his desk when Marc returned. It had not been the kind of long, vinous lunch that made businessmen who indulged in them perform at reduced efficiency for the rest of the working day. He was back by two-fifteen, with some speedwriting notes of his own for her to type.

The late afternoon brought a stream of faxes and telexes from Canada and North America, where the working day was just beginning.

It was after six when Marc's PC played the opening bars of what Sophie recognised as a violin concerto by Vivaldi as a reminder.

'I must go,' he said.

He had shown her his engagement diaries, the desk diary duplicated on his computer. She knew that tonight he was going to a reception at the German Embassy, an attractive building, painted yellow, on the north side of the wooden bridge between the smart part of town and the Accademia, where many of the city's greatest art treasures were housed.

As he was leaving the room Marc said, 'Tomorrow we're going to Torcello. I suggest you wear a cotton frock. We'll be lunching at the Locanda Cipriani and it can be very warm in the garden there at midday.'

'Why are we going to Torcello?' She had planned to visit the island on her first free day. She didn't want anyone with her the first time she went back.

'The grandmother of one of my college friends arrived in Venice this morning. I'm under an obligation to show her some of the sights and Torcello isn't too taxing for someone in her eighties. You can help me entertain her.'

'Wouldn't your cousin be a better choice?'

'Chiara has been to Torcello too many times to find it an interesting excursion . . . unless it's with a new boyfriend. She's not interested in anyone in Mrs Henderson's age group. I don't suppose you are either, but you'll make a better job of pretending to enjoy being with her. See you tomorrow.'

When he crossed the large room the way his hair flicked into half-curls just above his shirt-collar and the jut of his cheekbone rang a faint bell in her mind, like a muted and hard-to-hear version of the musical reminder that Marc had had installed on his PC.

Then, as he disappeared, the clouded memory cleared. She knew where they had met before. How could she have forgotten? Except that the brain had a way of blotting out days and events too painful to recall.

CHAPTER EIGHT

IN ORDER to have some time on the island before the famous restaurant opened its doors to those who could afford to lunch there, they collected Mrs Henry Henderson from her hotel at eleven o'clock.

Marc left Sophie in the launch while he went inside the hotel. On his advice she was wearing a summer frock, but it was a conservative style with not too much bare flesh on view. The parts that were bare she had covered with a high-protection sun lotion, knowing that travelling by water increased the danger of burning. She hadn't left off her tights in case Mrs Henderson had old-fashioned, old-money ideas, and didn't approve of bare legs in elegant restaurants.

Although she had lived nearby for a long stretch of her life, Sophie had never entered the Locanda Cipriani, but Torcello received many famous visitors, both to see its church and to lunch at the *locanda*. Before Sophie's time, the Queen of England had been there and, after her time there, Prince Charles. The list of celebrities was long, including the American writer Ernest Hemingway, who had taken a room at the *locanda* to shoot duck and write a novel.

But the life Sophie had lived there with Michael had had no connection with all the comings and goings of the world's VIPs. Although, out of curiosity, she had planned to eat lunch at the *locanda* when she returned to the island, she hadn't expected to travel on a private launch, and would have preferred to be going by ferry.

When Marc reappeared with his guest, Sophie blinked. Could this slender and upright woman in a white voile shirt and white cotton trousers, with a broad-brimmed dark green straw hat in her hand, be an eighty-year-old?

Stepping lightly into the launch, with a gracious '*Buon giorno... molto grazie*' for the boatman who gave her his hand, she said to Sophie, 'Isn't this a perfect morning? I'm Martha Henderson.'

Sophie had risen and was standing braced to keep her balance and to steady the American if, as Marc came abroad, the launch lurched under his weight.

'How do you do, Mrs Henderson?'

'Please call me Martha. I don't like to be formal,' she said, with a smile.

What a breathtaking beauty she must have been in her youth, thought Sophie. As indeed she still was, but not with the artificially preserved looks of many of her American contemporaries. There were no detectable signs that Martha had kept age at bay with surgery and long hours spent with beauticians. Her hair was white, her make-up minimal, her jewellery proclaiming her style rather than her wealth. It was her supple waist, her visible *joie de vivre* and her delicious light scent which made her seem ageless: a woman who had lived a long time but was still finding life an adventure.

That Marc was having similar thoughts was shown by the look he exchanged with Sophie while Mrs Henderson was settling herself and lifting her face to the sun with closed eyes and a wordless murmur of pleasure.

'I came here on my first honeymoon in 1936,' she told Sophie as they moved off. 'Marc tells me you arrived a few days ago. Aren't you overwhelmed by all this beauty? Don't you envy people who spend their lives here?'

'Yes, I do,' Sophie said truthfully.

'When I was here with James, my first husband, I wanted to stay. I wanted to re-plan our future. But for him that was impossible. He was a lawyer, like his father and grandfather. He had his life all mapped out and I couldn't ask him to change it. Then the war came and changed many lives, including ours.'

They were passing the Palazzo Non Finito, the unfinished building which would have been the largest palace on the canal had it been completed. Now its single white marble storey bore a sign: 'Peggy Guggenheim Collection'.

'I met her once,' Martha said. 'I envied her living in Venice for thirty years. She had one of the last privately owned gondolas, you know. But I didn't envy her private life. She must often have been very lonely. Did your grandfather know her well, Marc?'

He was sitting on the other side of her, at right angles to the two women sharing the comfortably cushioned stern seat. The breeze was ruffling his hair.

'Yes, but he disliked her collection of modern art so they were never close friends.'

'I don't like most of it either, but I do like the Marini statue of the horseman we'll see through the water-gates. When you come out of the house and walk round and see his erection, it's such a shock the first time. Was that the artist's motive, do you suppose? To shock people? I wonder if the story is true that one day, when a group of nuns were coming to visit unexpectedly, Peggy unscrewed the penis and threw it in the canal?' She turned to Sophie. 'Have you seen it?'

Marc answered for her. 'She hasn't had time to visit any galleries yet. And Sophie has too much aplomb to be shocked by anything,' he added blandly.

He must know that wasn't true, Sophie thought, clenching her teeth. He had rocked her aplomb several times.

Martha looked closely at her. 'You do look a very calm person. What's your secret? Yoga and meditation?'

Considering how tense she was feeling about going back to Torcello, Sophie was amazed that she gave Mrs Henderson an impression of serenity, especially as she felt sure there had been nothing tongue-in-cheek about the American's comment.

'Walking and reading are my main relaxations,' she said quietly.

'Oh, mine too.' In a spontaneous gesture, Martha stretched out her hand to give Sophie's wrist a friendly squeeze. 'I haven't "measured out my life with coffee spoons". It's been a long country walk marked by a trail of books.' After a pause, she added, 'I might have that on my tombstone. What do you think, Marc?'

'I like it.' He was smiling at Martha with a look that caused curious sensations in the region of Sophie's heart. 'But if tombstones can have postscripts I think I would add, "A very short time in her company made you feel you had found a friend."'

Mrs Henderson looked delighted. As well she might, Sophie thought.

'What a charming thing to say. I feel the same.' This time it was his arm she squeezed. She was obviously a very tactile person. 'But I've heard a lot of good things about you from Hal.' She turned to Sophie. 'I had four children with my first husband and two more when I married again, after the war. Now I have a whole tribe of grandchildren. Hal is the eldest grandson. He's the same age as Marc—thirty-six. When he was eighteen, he had a terrible accident on his motorbike. It left him a paraplegic. He's married now, with two children, but at first it was very difficult for an active young man like him to adapt to life in a wheelchair. Marc helped him make that adjustment.'

'He exaggerates my contribution,' said Marc. 'It was Hal's own determination which got him through his time in hospital and the first years at Yale.'

'He says it was you who did that—cheering him up when he was low, spending your free time with him instead of having a ball with the others.'

'I liked him better than the others. Why did I never meet you before?' Marc asked.

Sophie liked the deft way he turned the conversation away from himself.

'My second husband was ill while Hal was at Yale. We were living in France and I wasn't around much then. That's a lovely hotel. That's where I stayed the second time I came here.' She gestured at the Danieli, a luxurious near-neighbour of Sophie's more modest base.

Further along the Riva, they turned down the canal which led to the Arsenale. As they glided through the lion-guarded water-gate into what had once been the largest shipyard in the world, Sophie remembered coming this way with Michael on the *vaporetto*, the only way for members of the public to see inside the walls of the Arsenale. He had wanted to paint the vast caverns of the covered docks but hadn't been able to get permission.

Marc had turned to look at something to starboard, and was showing the same quarter-profile which, yesterday afternoon, had unlocked her memory of their first encounter. If he was thirty-six now, when she'd been eleven he would have been twenty-two.

At the time he had seemed very adult, but he might still have been a student, visiting Venice on vacation. If he hadn't been there and known what to do, Michael would have died. *She* hadn't known what to do.

'The first time I came to Torcello was by gondola,' said Martha as they approached the island. The bell-tower of its ancient cathedral had been in view for some time.

'In those days you could hire a gondola, with two gondoliers to row it, for a whole day for very little. I remember we brought a picnic. It was almost dark by the time we got back to Venice. It was one of the best days of my life.'

'Aren't you nervous about coming back?' Sophie asked.

Martha gave a gentle shake of the head. 'Whatever it's like now it can't spoil that wonderful memory. They sang to us on the way back. They didn't have very good voices but even so it was lovely. There was a full moon rising and Venice looked like Camelot or Atlantis—one of those legendary places you expect to vanish as you approach it.'

'Does your gondolier sing, Sophie?' Marc enquired.

'I don't know,' she said untruthfully.

Perhaps Martha heard a nuance that alerted her curiosity. With an interested look, she said, 'Who is your gondolier?'

'He's someone Marc thinks picked me up,' Sophie told her pleasantly. 'But he happens to have an aunt who runs a very good restaurant and a large friendly family who are only too happy to let me listen in to their conversations in the Venetian dialect. Being able to speak it will be a help in dealing with local people, especially working people.'

'She omits to mention that her gondolier is too handsome for his own good and has the reputation of seducing every susceptible tourist who comes within a hundred yards of him.'

Marc was smiling as he said it, but something in his eyes reminded her of the expression on a cat's face when, with claws temporarily sheathed, it dabbed a soft paw against a terrified mouse or captured fledgling.

Controlling her indignation, she said, 'Do you have grounds for that statement?'

'One of Domenico's cousins is a gondolier. They all know each other. There are only about four hundred of them left.' He turned to Martha. 'Apparently Sophie's guy is well-known for targeting the cream of the foreign girls... with close to a hundred per cent success rate, so I'm told.'

'Well, he isn't targeting *me*,' Sophie retorted, losing some of her cool. And then, already strung up and resenting being needled, she repeated what, long ago, she had heard a Venetian girl from one of the poorer quarters say to a man who had been annoying her.

The words were no sooner spoken than she was horrified, and thankful that Mrs Henderson, even if she had some Italian, was unlikely to have understood the coarseness of her terse instruction to mind his own business and push off.

For a moment Marc's face was blank, and she had a sinking feeling he was going to dismiss her there and then. It was an enormous relief when he began to laugh.

'Is that what he's taught you to say if anyone else makes a pass at you? It would certainly have an effect. But ask yourself this: would you say the English equivalent if someone in New York or London was making a nuisance of himself? I doubt it.' He glanced at Martha. 'Don't ask me to translate Sophie's pithy mouthful. Those words aren't in your vocabulary.'

'They might not be in my personal vocabulary, but I expect I've heard them spoken or read them in books,' Martha said drily. 'I don't think I'm behind the times. I try not to be. But one thing I do dislike about contemporary manners is the way both sexes swear in front of each other.' She turned to Sophie. 'I'm sure *you* don't, my dear... except to give Marc an example of the Venetian you've learnt,' she added, with a mischievous look.

The launch was slowing down to pass the jetty where the ferry passengers disembarked. It was near the mouth of a small canal and the footpath leading to the centre of the island.

Her attention distracted by the cut and thrust with Marc, it was only now that Sophie looked at the jetty. She had so often stood there with Michael, waiting for the boat to Venice where he, with the sleeve of his missing right arm neatly folded and pinned to the side of his shirt, had earned their living drawing portraits of tourists with his left hand.

Martha gave an exclamation. 'The path has been paved with bricks. It was a dirt path last time.'

To Sophie, the other woman's voice seemed to come from a long way away. She was looking past the jetty, to the spot where *Venezia* had once been moored.

Michael had given his boat the Italian name for Venice long before he'd come to Torcello. He had loved the city all his life, but before losing his arm had been busy working in London, where he had been one of the great fashion artists of his day.

Behind the protective screen of her sunglasses, Sophie closed her eyes for a moment. When she opened them the launch had entered the canal. The painful sight of *Venezia's* empty mooring had passed out of view.

The path alongside the canal had been paved with bricks laid in a herring-bone pattern.

'That's much prettier than concrete or asphalt,' said Martha.

The pattern reminded Sophie of the paths in the walled kitchen garden of her English boarding-school—a great country house once owned by an aristocratic family which had died out.

Shortly before his death, Michael had inherited some money—enough to send her to boarding-school and to cover her education until she was eighteen and could start supporting herself. At first she had been very unhappy away from him, but every week a letter illustrated with funny sketches had arrived to cheer her up until, gradually, she had grown to like her new environment and to throw herself into doing well and making him proud of her.

The launch glided under a bridge without any parapets. A young couple who looked as if they might be honeymooners were sitting on it. Sophie wondered if they would be a poignant reminder to Martha's of her first visit here. But everything must remind her of that long-lost happiness. It sounded as if her first husband had been killed in the war that Michael had also fought in.

'Did you come here as a child, Marc?' the older woman asked.

He nodded. 'My grandfather liked to lunch here whenever he was in Venice. He knew Guiseppe Cipriani, the founder of Harry's Bar and the Cipriani Hotel, and Guiseppe knew everyone from Winston Churchill to Charlie Chaplin and Sophia Loren. I should think the *locanda* here has welcomed more celebrated people than any other inn of its size in the world.'

Several elderly women had set up stalls selling lace and hand-embroidered linens on the path between the rustic inn and the eleventh-century church built as a shrine to a forgotten saint. The cathedral behind it was even older, its interior adorned with wonderful mosaics. Michael had often sat there, gazing at the tall black-robed Madonna, with Sophie sitting quietly beside him, trying to imagine Torcello as it had been long ago: the most important island in the lagoon, with more than ten thousand inhabitants and many churches and convents.

Today the ancient cathedral was full of visitors, and she couldn't recapture the sense of awe and mystery she had felt in this place as a child. Perhaps Martha also found the presence of other people an intrusion on her memories. They did not stay long.

A deferential young man welcomed them to the *locanda* and ushered them into a garden from which the roofs of the two churches were visible above the surrounding trees.

'Would the ladies prefer a table in the shade?' he asked Marc.

Marc looked inquiringly at them.

'I like the sun, but I have a shady hat,' said Martha. 'Is the sun too strong for you, Sophie? You're very fair-skinned.'

'I love the sun too. I shan't burn. I have lashings of sun cream on.'

'How sensible of you,' said Martha as they were shown to one of the tables in full sunlight. 'But I guess good sense is an essential qualification for your job. I often wonder how I'd have got on in the business world, but my parents were comfortably off and when I was twenty James swept into my life, so I've never had to earn my living.'

'You raised six useful members of the next generation,' said Marc, watching her put on her green hat.

Sophie listened with half an ear to their easy flow of conversation. She was looking about her, taking in the details of a place which had once seemed as inaccessible to her as a fairy-tale palace to a woodcutter's grand-daughter. Not that Michael had been the modern equivalent of a woodcutter, but they had been almost as poor as the peasants in the tales he had read to her when she'd been little.

The tables had blue cloths, a paler blue than the vivid sky overhead, and the part of the garden she was facing was planted with pomegranate bushes, their bright red fruit peeping out of the foliage. Soon all the tables were taken, and the waiters, their shoes crunching on the gravel underfoot, bustled back and forth with menus, bottles of wine in buckets of ice and baskets of shell-shaped rolls.

When Marc and the two women had made their de-
cisions about what to eat and were sipping chilled white
wine, Martha said thoughtfully, 'I wonder what happened on this island to change it from the way it was in
the tenth century to the way it is now? Was it struck by
the plague?'

'The current theory,' said Marc, 'is that the action of
two rivers caused the waters surrounding the island to
become a malarial swamp. Most people don't realise how
shallow the lagoon is…less than two feet in most places.'

He began to talk about the conflict between the needs
of the region's human inhabitants and its wildlife, and
it was clear he was a knowledgeable student of the
problems involved.

Much of what he told Martha about the plant and
bird life Sophie already knew, and as she listened her
thoughts drifted back to the day they had met for the
first time…

'I'm feeling a bit below par. I think I'll take the day off,'
Michael announced after breakfast.

'Yes, why don't you?' Sophie agreed, trying not to
show her concern.

For some time past she had suspected that her grandfather wasn't well. His energy had diminished. He was
often tired. Sometimes he was short of breath. But when
she'd suggested a check-up he'd dismissed the idea and
claimed to be perfectly well and just beginning to feel
his age.

He had married late, and when Sophie had come into
his care, at the age of three, was already in his sixties.
For most of his life he had been one of the world's top
fashion artists, ranking with Eric, Bouché and Gruau,
discovered by *Vogue* while he was still at art school and
remaining a frequent contributor to their pages and those
of other glossy magazines for several decades.

Three factors had contributed to his becoming a street artist in Venice. In the sixties drawings had lost favour with fashion editors, and then an accident had resulted in the loss of his arm. In the seventies his son and daughter-in-law had died in an Atlantic storm. He had been living in Venice at the time, with his boat in a nearby marina, and for the next few years he and his grandchild had moved from hotel to hotel, each one cheaper than the last. Eventually they had taken to living on the boat, their funds still steadily dwindling.

In competition with many local artists trying to eke a living selling picturesque views to the tourists, he augmented his income by drawing exaggerated portraits with his left hand.

Three times a week, throughout the steadily expanding tourist season, he spent all day on the Riva, taking Sophie with him. She did not go to school but was given lessons by Michael. By living abroad they escaped any intervention from what he called 'interfering busybodies', whether official or otherwise.

Michael spent the morning quietly, but soon after lunch could not hide his breathlessness. He admitted to having unpleasant sensations in his chest and went to lie down. Presently she heard him groan and went into his cabin to find him, grey-faced and sweating, with a pain shooting up his arm.

'I think I'm having a heart attack.' He began to shiver.

Sophie tucked a blanket round him and fetched the pillow from her cabin. 'I'll go and get help. Don't move. Don't exert yourself.'

Panic-stricken, but trying to keep calm, she hurried on deck and sprang ashore, scanning the channel in both directions in the hope of seeing a fast boat which could transport Michael to hospital. But there was nothing to be seen but the wide expanses of reed beds and sky-reflecting water.

The only option was to run like a hare to the *locanda* and ask them to telephone for a water ambulance. Or, with luck, there might still be a *motoscafo* there—one of the expensive water taxis which brought tourists who could afford them to visit the island.

She was only a short way along the path leading to the *locanda* when she saw a motorboat coming towards her. Waving both arms, Sophie shouted, *'Aiuto! Aiuto!'*

After her first rush of relief, she realised the boat wasn't a taxi but a private craft, with a group of good-looking young Italians on board. For a minute she feared they might ignore her and sweep past, not wanting to be bothered with someone in trouble. Even if they did stop, she wasn't hopeful that they would know how to deal with the contingency. They looked the sort Michael had once called *jeunesse dorée*, meaning literally 'gilded youth'. His tone had implied that such people were generally spoilt and selfish pleasure-seekers.

Only one of them noticed her: the young man at the wheel. He cut the throttle and brought the boat alongside. 'What's the matter, kid?'

CHAPTER NINE

'IT'S an emergency. My grandfather's having a heart attack. Please help me.'

The young man turned to the others, his sharp, 'Be quiet, you lot!' stopping their laughter and chatter as abruptly as he had cut the purr of the motor. 'Where is the old boy?' he asked her.

'In our boat . . . round the corner—on the far side of the ferry-stop.'

'Make room and give her a hand,' the young man said to another sitting behind him. 'She can perch on your lap for a minute.'

In other circumstances Sophie might have been shy of sitting on a stranger's lap. But now her only concern was getting back to Michael, who might already be dead.

When the motorboat reached *Venezia*'s mooring it took the young man at the wheel only seconds to make his boat fast to a mooring ring with a quick clove hitch. Sophie, who had also leapt ashore, grabbed his arm.

'You'll need help to move him to your boat. He's a big man . . . as tall as you are. They'll have to get out. There won't be room for him otherwise.'

'Calm down, kid. It won't help to panic.'

He headed for *Venezia*.

Michael was where she had left him. At first she thought he was dead and her own heart seemed to stop. Then the eyes in the grey face opened.

'Who the devil are you?' he asked in English, in a faint wheezing voice Sophie had never heard before.

'Take it easy, sir. We'll take care of you.'

103

To Sophie's surprise, the young man spoke perfect English.

To her, he said, 'You stay here and reassure him. Luckily I brought my cellphone. I'll call the nearest medic. There may be one on Burano.'

She followed him out of the cabin, saying in an urgent undertone, 'He needs more than a doctor. He needs to be taken to hospital.'

The young man whipped round to face her. He was wearing a spotless white T-shirt, jeans with bright scarlet braces and a red and white neckerchief round his long suntanned neck. He smelt nice, of soap and the stuff men put on their faces after shaving. Michael had used it once but could no longer afford it. These days he didn't shave much, or wash as often as he used to when she was smaller. He didn't smell clean any more, but always faintly musty.

The young man put both hands on her shoulders, saying quietly but with assurance, 'When someone's having a heart attack the best thing to do is *not* move them. That could do more harm than good. Let him stay where he is and we'll get a doctor to him. He'll need medication before he's taken to hospital. It's a long way from here.'

Seeing the lingering doubt in her eyes, he added, 'More than eighty per cent of the people who survive the first few hours after a heart attack get better. He'll pull through. He looks a tough old guy.'

Sophie was roused from her memories by the arrival of her first course.

'You were a long way away then,' said Marc.

Embarrassed that he had noticed, she said, 'I'm sorry...something you said took me back to my childhood.' She didn't add that, although it was far back in time, in distance the place where she had been was very near where she was now.

'I'm reaching the age when my childhood often seems clearer than what happened a few years ago,' said Martha. 'Tell me some more about *your* island, Marc. How long will it take you to make it the way you want it?'

'Probably the rest of my life. I should feel a lot happier if I'd been able to buy it, but the lease is a long one and my lawyers managed to negotiate an option to renew.'

As he summarised his plans for the island, which Sophie had already heard, she tried to analyse the difference between his face as it was now and as it had looked the first time their lives had converged.

The second and last time she had seen him had been at the hospital, late in the evening of the day Michael had been admitted. She'd been sitting on a bench in a corridor, waiting for news from the intensive care ward, when the young man had appeared, this time wearing a white dinner jacket with his dark hair tidy instead of wind-blown.

He had brought her a bag of books to help her pass the time and asked if they had fixed her up with somewhere to spend the night. She had told him about Paolo's family, who would let her sleep at their house.

At the end of their conversation the young man had said, 'Tomorrow I have to leave Venice. I'll look you up next time I'm here. You'll be back on your boat by then, I expect. I'm glad I was around to help out. *Arrivederci.*'

But perhaps by the time he'd returned he had forgotten about her as, after a while, she had succeeded in forgetting him—or at least in putting him and that day so far to the back of her mind that it hadn't been until yesterday that she had made the connection between him and the man now sitting opposite.

'Do I have a blob of sauce on my chin, Sophie?' Marc asked.

'What? Oh...was I staring? I'm sorry.'

'You're *distraite* today,' he said drily. 'First you go off in a trance, then you fix me with a stare like a cobra preparing to strike. What's on your mind?'

'Nothing...nothing at all.'

She pulled herself together and spent the rest of the meal attending to what was said and showing her appreciation of what she was eating.

'If you two feel like a stroll,' said Martha, replacing her coffee-cup in its saucer, 'I'd like to go back to the cathedral and listen to the audio-guide on one of those telephone gadgets we saw people using this morning. Such things hadn't been invented when I was here before.'

Marc signalled for the bill. 'Tomorrow, if you decide to revisit the Doge's Palace, you'll find they now have portable audio-guides that not only describe the room you're in and its paintings but allow you to backtrack or to move along faster than other people. That's a big improvement on the regular guided tour, don't you think?'

'It's a brilliant idea,' she agreed. 'I've never liked guided tours, especially not the kind where the guide holds up an umbrella so that you won't lose sight of her or tag along with another guide's group by mistake. Tomorrow I may not do any sightseeing. I may just potter around, shopping and sitting in Florian's, watching the world go by.'

Sophie knew that a stroll with Marc would offer the perfect opportunity to reveal to him that she knew Venice better than he realised. However, now that she had remembered their previous meeting, she was curious to see if, before they left Torcello, he would suddenly slot her into place as the scruffy child he had helped.

She had changed far more than he, but not out of all recognition. Her eyes hadn't changed. Surely, when they passed the place where *Venezia* had been moored, if she lingered there he would remember her?

When Martha had disappeared inside the cathedral, they took a path Sophie knew passed by some fields and eventually wound in a loop.

She said, 'In spite of her age, I think Mrs Henderson must be one of the most glamorous people who ever lunched at the *locanda*. She looks wonderful in that green hat.'

'She has great style,' he agreed. 'You'll look that way too at her age. Women with beautiful eyes always age well.'

His tone was so matter-of-fact that it didn't seem like a compliment. She let it pass without acknowledgement. But it lit a small inner glow she doused by reminding herself that it might be something he had said to a lot of girls.

'I once stayed here overnight,' Marc told her. 'They have a few simple rooms. When the last visitors had gone home, it was unbelievably peaceful.'

I know. I've been here at dusk and at night. The words were on the tip of her tongue. For some reason, she didn't say them.

They walked on in silence, Sophie a little ahead because the path was narrow. This was the way she had always come back to *Venezia* after fetching the makings of soup from the islanders who had sold them vegetables. Soup, and bread from the bakery on Burano, the lace-makers' island, had been their staple diet, with dried beans their main source of protein.

'Have you ever imagined living in a place like this for the rest of your life?' Marc asked, from behind her.

She could have said, I don't need to imagine it. I know what it's like living here. But again she held back. 'If I didn't have to earn my living, and given the right sort of companionship and an adequate supply of books, I can imagine being very happy here.'

'What do you mean by the right sort of companionship?' he asked.

'Most people can't live like hermits. They need conversation . . . affection. To live here always, I'd need a husband and children.'

'Are they part of your life plan?'

'They're on my wish list. That's a different thing from a plan. A plan is achievable. For a wish to come true it is more a matter of chance.'

'A wish has a better chance of coming true if the conditions are right for it.'

They had come to a wider stretch of path where two people could walk abreast. As he came alongside her Sophie looked up at him. 'What do you mean?'

'In the context of what we're discussing, you would have to recognise that your career plan and your wish list are likely to be incompatible. For example, if I needed you to work late and your gondolier had laid on a special date, you couldn't do both. You'd have to decide whose displeasure was more important.'

Sophie halted, turning to face him. 'Let's get this straight,' she said evenly. 'Paolo isn't a boyfriend. He's a friend, period. And if I had been invited to a big family party on a night when you wanted me to work I'd send his parents my apologies. Which isn't to say that I would *always* put work first.'

'Hold still a minute. You have something in your hair.' He stepped closer to remove it.

She drew in her breath, suddenly aware that warm sunlight, vintage wine and standing as close as this to an attractive male was a volatile combination. Was he also aware of it, or was it only she who felt all her senses sharpen?

'A small spider.' He spread his hand to show her the minute insect running down his middle finger. 'It must have dropped out of that overhanging branch we passed.'

The spider stopped when it reached the dark hairs on the back of his shapely brown hand. Marc looked at it for a moment, and then he moved close to a bush and gently blew it off his hand into the foliage.

'In what circumstances would you put it second?' he asked.

For a moment the question made no sense. The feelings she had experienced while he had been extricating the spider from her hair had temporarily wiped out all memory of their conversation. With an effort, she switched off her senses and murmured, 'Well...' playing for time while she re-set her mind.

'If I had any close relations and one of them was very ill, not expected to live, then they would definitely come first.'

'Your parents are dead, I believe? Were you born late in their lives?'

'On the contrary. My mother was only nineteen, my father twenty-four. He was a dedicated yachtsman and taught her to sail. When I was three they were both drowned. My father's father brought me up. It was a great grief to him, but not for me. My childhood was very happy.'

She was going to tell him more about it, but Marc intervened, saying, 'So was I—raised by my grandfather. He and I had everything in common, but he and his son were at loggerheads all their lives.'

'Did he disapprove of your father marrying an Italian girl?'

'Emphatically...and with reason. He suspected an ulterior motive and he was right. My mother wanted money, preferably dollars, to restore the *palazzo* and permit her to run accounts at all the best shops in Europe.

When my father recognised her motives, he stepped up his drinking. It can kill you surprisingly quickly, if you work at it. But Grandfather more than made up for their deficiencies as parents. Like you, I didn't grow up with any hang-ups...or none that I recognise,' he added drily.

She was surprised he should confide these intimate details to her. She would have expected him to be impenetrably reserved about things that mattered to him, as his father's drinking must have mattered when he was very young and when he had probably had a child's tendency to assume that if anything went wrong it must somehow be his fault.

By now they were approaching *Venezia*'s mooring, but instead of being deserted, like the field path, the towpath was dotted with tourists taking a stroll while waiting for the ferry.

A woman approached them, smiling. 'Could I trouble you to take a picture of me and my husband?' In case they didn't speak English, she mimed what she wanted.

'With pleasure.'

Marc took her camera and waited until she had posed herself with the man whose legs were pale varicose stalks between his shorts and the tops of his grey city socks.

After looking through the viewfinder, Marc said, 'Where you're standing, the campanile on Burano appears to be growing out of your head, sir. Move a little to your right.'

The photograph taken, the couple were disposed to chat. Marc wasn't. He moved Sophie on with a firm hand on her arm and a pleasant but brisk goodbye to the tourists.

'Given the smallest encouragement, they would have regaled us with details of all their trips to foreign parts,' he murmured, some yards further on.

'That's a little unkind,' she answered.

'I can be very unkind. I thought you knew that.' He was still holding her arm.

'You weren't unkind to the spider.'

'Spiders are never bores. People frequently are. If I'd been by myself I should have refused to be a party to the boredom they're going to inflict on their friends when they show them their holiday snaps. But that would have embarrassed you, wouldn't it?'

'Yes,' she admitted, with a smiling upward glance. 'But I think you're teasing me. You're too...gentlemanly to inflict pain on a harmless couple like that pair.'

'You think so, do you?' His tone implied she was being naïve to credit him with any finer instincts.

Their glances locked; his dark eyes amused, hers defensive. What was it about this man which made her feel as exposed as the crabs in the lagoon at the time when they cast off their shells?

This time it was he who suddenly checked his stride, tightening his fingers so that she also had to come to a standstill. Disconcerted by the intensity of his gaze, she said, 'Why are you staring at me?'

Had he recognised her?

CHAPTER TEN

MARC said, 'Tia Clara has an aquamarine ring she doesn't often wear. Held up to the sun, it would be the same colour as your irises. They're very unusual . . . very beautiful.'

Unaware that he had made her heart pound as violently as it had the day when, very near here, she had begged him for help, he glanced at his watch. 'We'd better get a move on. Martha will be wondering where we've got to.'

Mrs Henderson was sitting in the shade of the *locanda's* vine-shaded veranda, talking to a white-haired man in shorts and walking boots. His arms and legs were deeply bronzed. A day-pack was slung on the back of his chair.

'Professor, these are two friends of mine—Sophie Hill and Marc Washington. Professor Grant is staying at my hotel, Marc. I've suggested he rides back with us instead of taking the ferry.'

The professor's slight accent proclaimed him to be a Scot. Marc's civil interest in him revealed he had held the chair in archaeology at more than one university.

The two men spent much of the return journey discussing thermoluminescence and other esoteric matters Marc seemed to know about.

The two women didn't contribute to this conversation. Martha looked around her at the changing views of the lagoon, and Sophie put on a show of listening to whoever was speaking while actually studying their faces. They were not unlike in the height and breadth of their

112

foreheads and general angularity of feature. Both looked formidably intelligent.

Mark was clearly a match for the professor, in general if not specialist knowledge. It was obvious the older man found him stimulating company, and the fact that Marc made no effort to include Martha and herself in their talk made Sophie wonder if he had had enough of female society for one day and, during their walk, had begun to find himself bored.

She had not said anything scintillating, that was for sure. But then neither had he. It had been the exchange of personal background and perspective that people made when they were still in the early stages of getting to know each other.

A few minutes before they arrived back at Martha's hotel, he said, 'I have a couple of things to do downtown. I'll get off here. I'm not sure how long I'll be. I'll call you in half an hour.'

Back at the *palazzo*, Sophie checked the fax, telex and E-mail messages, played back some local messages on the answering machine and looked at the world news update on teletext. By the time Marc called she had made notes of everything he might want to know about immediately. There was nothing of crucial importance.

'Right,' he said, after hearing the summary, 'in that case you can go home, but I'd like you to be in the office by eight tomorrow. OK?'

'Of course . . . and thank you very much for including me in the trip to Torcello. It was a delicious lunch.'

'I'm glad you enjoyed it.' He rang off.

Walking back to the hotel, once stepping into the doorway of a shop when she saw a large tour group streaming down the narrow street ahead of her, Sophie wondered if she had only imagined a note of coolness in Marc's response to her thanks.

Usually she avoided the Piazza, with its throngs of camera-happy visitors, but today she decided to have tea at Quadri's and listen to the music for an hour before buying some fruit and a carton of yogurt for a light supper in her room to counterbalance the lavish lunch.

The afternoon shadows from the surrounding buildings with their elegant arcades of luxury shops reached the tables outside Quadri's later than at Caffè Florian, the coffee-house favoured by the Venetian élite, who had been meeting their friends there since 1720.

Florian's was also popular with artists, but on the rare occasions when he had been able to afford to drink and draw the passing throng in the Piazza Michael had preferred Quadri's.

Knowing she was going to pay through the nose for the privilege, Sophie chose a table and ordered tea. Behind her, on a canopied dais, a group of musicians led by a violinist was playing a slightly jazzed-up version of a romantic melody she had first heard on Michael's wind-up gramophone.

Mostly it had been classical music echoing across the lagoon from *Venezia*'s deck. But one or two of the records had been collections of evergreen love songs. Hearing one of them now moved her almost to tears.

In her teens she had never doubted that in a few years' time she would find her own Mr Wonderful and be as happy with him as her grandmother and mother had been with the men they'd loved.

But it hadn't happened. Twice she had started relationships which hadn't fulfilled her hopes. Now here she was, with another birthday approaching and still on her own, in a place where loneliness had an extra poignancy. Anywhere as magical as Venice needed to be shared with someone special. Where was her special person? Did he even exist, except in her mind?

'*Signorina...*'

As the waiter arranged her tea things—a cup and saucer, a pot of hot water, Earl Grey teabags, slices of lemon and a bill which she knew would include a hefty supplement for the music—his wedding ring glinted in the sunlight. When he finished his shift there would be someone waiting to spend the evening with him. Probably Martha and the professor would have dinner together. Everyone seemed to be in pairs. Except me, thought Sophie forlornly.

A pair of hands came from behind her and covered her eyes. She knew it had to be Paolo. This was what he had done long ago, when they'd been children.

'I don't have to guess. I know. Why aren't you working?'

He removed his hands and took the chair next to hers. 'I have to take some time off. Aren't you pleased to see me?'

'I was enjoying the music...now you'll want me to listen to you,' she said lightly.

'When I've ordered a drink, I won't say another word.' He beckoned a waiter. 'We will sit in silence, like old people who have said everything they have to say to each other.'

Somewhat to Sophie's surprise, he kept his promise. Ten minutes later they were still sitting in silence, Paolo sipping his *ombra* and watching the pigeons strut back and forth, undisturbed by the people crossing the Piazza but sometimes taking refuge in the air when a child tried to sneak up on them.

At last, taking pity on him, Sophie said, 'I should think that's the longest you've ever been quiet in your life, isn't it? Your mother would never believe me if I told her you'd kept your mouth shut for a quarter of an hour.'

'Mamma has warned me against you,' Paolo informed her. 'She's afraid you will break my heart. You think I'm joking? It's true. She wants me to settle down with a nice local girl, not waste my time with a foreign career girl like you. It's not that she doesn't like you. She does ... very much. But she wants a daughter-in-law who will be happy in Venice and give her two or three grandchildren—as if she didn't have enough already.'

'Why does she think I wouldn't be happy in Venice? I grew up here ... or not far away.'

'But you've been to New York, London, Paris ... all those places she wanted to see before she married Babbo. She doesn't think Venice is anything special.'

'She would if she'd seen other places. The rest of the world has been ruined by cars. But she's right in seeing that we wouldn't suit each other. Even if you loved me, Paolo, you wouldn't be faithful to me. It's not your nature to want only one woman. For a while, perhaps, but not for the rest of your life.'

'Whether a man is faithful depends on his wife,' he said, with a shrug. 'Sometimes, after they're married, women lose interest in sex. They love their children more than their husbands. They wear nightgowns in bed.'

'In an old house with no central heating and snow on the roof, I'm not surprised,' she said drily. 'When I lived here, in winter we slept inside down sleeping bags.'

She remembered how cosy it had been, snuggled inside her bag, after Michael had kissed her goodnight, listening to the creaking of *Venezia*'s timbers and sometimes, according to the tide, the soft splash of water against the hull.

'Michael was old and you were a child,' said Paolo. 'If you slept with me I'd keep you warm with the heat from my body.' His look made it clear he was visualising the situation.

Sophie said briskly, 'The winters aren't long. In summer it's hot and humid. I should think most married people who can afford it have twin beds. Sharing a double can't be comfortable in August. Anyway, your mother is right. I'm a career girl, Paolo. Staying at home, having babies doesn't appeal to me.'

'I wouldn't make you stay at home. Between us we could afford to pay someone to look after the children.' He leaned towards her, seizing her hand. 'I've fallen for you, Sophie. I knew the night I took you home. Mamma saw what had happened to me.'

'Oh, Paolo—' Sophie began.

She broke off with a start as someone behind her said, *'Ciao.'*

It was Chiara, looking with undisguised curiosity at the man clasping Sophie's hand.

Paolo returned Chiara's interested smile with a scowl which made it clear that her presence was intrusive. But when, removing her hand from his, Sophie introduced them, he did stand up, albeit reluctantly and still with a far from friendly expression on his face.

Sophie's reaction to the Italian girl's arrival was mixed. She was glad to have Paolo's declaration of his feelings cut short, but thought it tactless of Chiara to butt in on what had all too clearly been a private conversation. Also, she didn't want it to get back to Marc that she had been holding hands with Paolo.

'Where did you two meet?' Chiara asked, dumping a shiny carrier bag from the Kenzo shop on the chair facing Sophie and seating herself in the one opposite Paolo.

To stop him from saying they had known each other as children—something else she didn't want Marc to learn from his cousin—Sophie said, 'Paolo is a gondolier.'

'Really?' Chiara put her elbows on the edge of the table and cupped her face in her hands. 'When I was ten I was in love with one of the gondoliers at Bacino Orseolo.' She gestured in the direction of the archway leading from the north-west corner of the Piazza to a pool which was one of the city's official gondola stations.

'Sometimes when I went past he would wink at me. He was younger than all the others and *very* handsome. But I never spoke to him. You're the first gondolier I've met.'

'That sounds like Bruno,' said Paolo. 'He had lots of schoolgirls in love with him.'

'He disappeared. What happened to him?'

'He came to a sticky end,' Paolo said, with a grimace. 'He left Venice to be a toy boy, then started drinking too much and perhaps doing drugs. Eventually he smashed himself up in the car his rich mistress had given him. He's back here now, but you wouldn't recognise him. He's an out-of-work wreck, kept by his mother. Anyone else would have left him to rot in the gutter.'

'How terrible!' Chiara looked devastated by this update on her girlhood idol.

Sophie thought it unkind of Paolo to have told her. She could imagine how shattered she would have felt on hearing a similar tale about the man with red braces who had saved Michael's life, leaving her with a memory of handsome young manhood that she had treasured for several years until, in the way of most teenage memories, it had been silted over by other experiences.

The waiter came. 'What would you like?' Paolo asked, perhaps regretting being the cause of Chiara's tragic expression.

She asked for a *cappuccino*. Sophie wondered if she would pay for it herself or expect him to.

'Who was the woman who took him away from Venice?' Chiara asked.

'Some millionaire's wife whose husband was too busy making money to worry about what she was doing. She came here to buy a gondola for a party on their private lake. She didn't realise a gondola isn't a boat anyone can row just like that.' He snapped his fingers. 'She had to hire a gondolier to go with it. Bruno wasn't the only one she approached, but he was the only one too stupid

to see the job involved more than rowing her gondola
for her.'

'Did she ask you?' asked Chiara.

'As a matter of fact, she did. I turned her down. She
was as old as my mother, even if she didn't look it.' He
put the tips of his forefingers at the sides of his eyes,
tightening the skin until his lids were taut slits.

'She sounds a horrible person.'

'You girls aren't the only ones who get passes made
at you,' Paolo told her. 'It happens to us all the time.'
He grinned. 'I've lost count of the ladies who have lost
their balance on purpose when I'm helping them out at
the end of their ride.'

'I'm sure they don't do that with all the gondoliers,'
said Chiara. 'Some of the ones I've noticed have been
anything but handsome.' She looked him over. 'You look
the way gondoliers are supposed to look.'

Paolo returned her appraisal. 'You look like a model.
Are you?'

Chiara shook her head. 'It's a job I wouldn't mind,
but my mother would have a fit.'

Her chair was facing the musicians' dais and the arcade
between the outside part of the *caffè* and the interior of
Quadri's. Suddenly she sat up straight, smiling and
waving to someone Paolo and Sophie couldn't see
without turning round.

'That was Marc,' she told Sophie. 'He's my cousin
and Sophie's boss,' she added, for Paolo's benefit.

'I've met him.'

'Life is more fun when he's here . . . as long as nothing
upsets him. Then he acts like a volcano.' She used her
expressive hands to mime a violent eruption.

Sophie wondered how he would react to seeing his
young, sheltered cousin hobnobbing with a gondolier—
especially a gondolier with Paolo's reputation.

As soon as she had finished her tea, she caught the waiter's eye. 'Your coffee's on me, Chiara,' she said, taking the bill for the *cappuccino* and giving the waiter a note to cover the totals on both slips.

'No, no... I'm paying,' said Paolo. He flourished a fifty thousand lire banknote which, to Sophie's concealed indignation, the waiter took instead of hers.

'Thank you.' Chiara gave Paolo a gracious smile.

'My pleasure.' He told her the name of his gondola station and added, 'Any time you fancy a ride, for you I'll make a special price. We're not supposed to charge less than the official minimum, but sometimes I do. Why not? It's my gondola.'

'You could find yourself losing your licence if you flirt with Chiara,' Sophie informed him when, after leaving Chiara at the *caffè*, they were walking in the direction of the Riva.

'I wasn't flirting. I was being friendly,' he answered. 'Are you jealous? That's a good sign.'

'Of course I'm not jealous,' she said shortly. 'I don't want my boss annoyed—which he would be if Chiara accepted your offer of a cut-price ride.'

'Nothing naughty can happen in a gondola unless it has a cabin,' Paolo said, laughing. '"The shelter of sweet sins". That was what your poet, Lord Byron, called the *felze*—and it was, in his time. Gondoliers had to turn a deaf ear to a lot of heavy breathing from inside *felzi* in the old days. Now we only use them during Carnival. Pity, really. There must be honeymoon couples who'd like to make love on a canal ride, if they could do it in private... and not only honeymooners. Most people would get a kick out of doing it in a gondola.'

Sophie ignored these remarks, walking as fast as was possible in an area always thronged with tourists, especially at the sunset hour. She was beginning to feel there was nowhere in the city where she was safe from

Paolo's unwanted courtship. She couldn't deny that there was a strong bond between them, but from her point of view it was fraternal, not romantic.

It was symptomatic of her mood that the crowd of sightseers on the Ponte della Paglia made her clench her teeth with exasperation as she edged her way through them with Paolo behind her.

On the other side, when the jostling throng had thinned out, she said to him, 'Are you on your way to see someone?'

'No, I'm coming with you. That's a nice dress for the daytime but you'll need something warmer as soon as the sun sets. You don't have to change in a hurry. I'll sit in the *caffè* and have another *ombra*.'

'Paolo, I can't have dinner with you tonight. I have things to do. I need some time to myself.'

'You're angry with me.'

His face had the same downcast look she had seen on it when, as a boy, he'd been given a verbal lashing by his mother for some misdeed she had discovered.

'I'm not angry, but I think it's foolish to talk about being in love with me. You may fancy me, but you haven't known me long enough to love me. You only know what I was like as a child. You don't know the person I am now.'

'Don't you believe in love at first sight?'

Sophie shook her head. 'I believe in attraction at first sight. But true love is different...it grows between people...it takes time.'

'For you, perhaps. Not for me. I've had a lot of girlfriends, but none of them made me feel the way you do, Sophie. This time it's serious with me. I was sweet on you when we were kids, when you were still flat-chested and people could mistake you for a boy. Except for your mouth. You always had a pretty mouth. But my mother threatened to kill me if I ever tried to kiss you...and I was afraid of your grandfather. Although he only had one arm he was a tough old fellow and he would have murdered anyone who laid a finger on you.'

Sophie was silent, surprised that Paolo had had such thoughts about her at a time when she, although aware how babies were made, and prepared for the changes adolescence would bring, had still been a child emotionally.

Later, when, reluctantly, Paolo had gone, resigned to the fact that he would have to be patient with her, she went up to her room, before remembering she still had to shop for the makings of her solitary supper.

That done, she moved the comfortable chair close to the open French window which had its wrought-iron balustrade too close to the frame for it to be called a balcony.

By now the crowds on the Riva had dispersed, and with them her earlier irritation. It wasn't like her to be edgy. She knew it had to do with Marc's passing along the arcade and seeing the three of them together. She wondered if he would refer to it in the morning and if she would ever be the cause of one of his explosions of anger.

She recognised that she was a little afraid of him. She had never been nervous of any previous employers. Why did Marc have that effect?

He was already at his desk when she arrived the next morning.

During the night reports and memos had come through from parts of the world where, now, people were taking their lunch breaks or the working day was nearly over. Marc had already dictated several long memos he wanted her to process and transmit to various destinations.

For three hours he kept her at full stretch, and he worked equally hard. She had already had glimpses of his phenomenal memory, but this morning she had a clear view of the dauntingly intelligent mind which, like his stride, allowed him easily to outpace most other people.

Sophie knew herself to be more than ordinarily bright, but she also knew she couldn't and wouldn't wish to cope with the load on his shoulders. He was operating at a stress level which eventually, for most men, took its toll in raised blood pressure, ulcers and heart problems. But, in spite of what his cousin had said about him, Marc appeared calm and relaxed.

It was she who, when a coffee-tray was brought up by one of the maids, was glad of a breathing space. A succession of tasks requiring all her concentration had made her forget the events of yesterday afternoon and the apprehensive state of mind in which she had come to work.

It was Marc who took charge of the coffee-pot. While filling both cups he said, 'I'm happy to see Chiara spending time with you, but her mother wouldn't have approved of the tea party *à trois* in the Piazza yesterday. All my aunts are incorrigible snobs. Chiara had a crush on a gondolier when she was at school. That was harmless. Another might not be.'

'My plan was to sit there alone, enjoying the music. Then Paolo saw me and later Chiara joined us. It was a situation there was no way to prevent. I knew you wouldn't like it,' said Sophie. 'Soon after you passed us I left, and so did he. I really don't think you need worry that he'll start a flirtation with her.'

'You know him better than I do, but perhaps I have more experience of human nature.' Marc's tone was cynical. 'Chiara could be the plainest girl in Italy and still attract men. She's that vulnerable species, an heiress. The word gets around.'

'I'm sure it hasn't reached Paolo and wouldn't excite him if it did. He could have stayed with her when I left. He passed up the opportunity,' Sophie said shortly. 'Believe it or not, there are people in the world who are content with what they have and don't want to latch onto richer people. If contentment could be measured, I wouldn't mind betting that Paolo's relations are every bit as happy as yours.'

Aware that she might have said too much, she was relieved when an incoming telephone call put an end to the conversation.

CHAPTER ELEVEN

THE day after Martha's departure, Sophie was in Marc's room, going through his schedule for the following month with him, when the man who cleaned the household's shoes and ran errands delivered a very large gift-wrapped box.

She assumed it was something Marc had ordered until the man said, 'For you, *signorina*.'

'There must be some mistake. I haven't ordered anything.'

'It's your name on the label.' He turned it over to show her.

'You're right. It's addressed to me. How odd. Well, I'll deal with it later. Would you leave it in my office, please?'

Marc intervened. 'No, leave it here, Luciano.' He smiled at Sophie. 'We aren't so busy you haven't time to open an exciting parcel.'

Wondering if it could be an extravagant gesture from Paolo, she undid the wrappings, trying not to tear the paper. The box inside was instantly recognisable. It came from Missoni, one of the shops to which Sophie had taken Martha to shop for presents for her granddaughters.

'It has to be from Martha. She shouldn't have done this.' Sophie turned back the layers of tissue, revealing a knitted garment in the distinctive and complex blend of colours which made Missoni's designs as recognisable and beautiful as a Tiepolo ceiling or a Canaletto painting.

125

She lifted it out; it was a hip-length jacket with a scarf collar, as warm as tweed but far more adaptable—the sort of glamorous, heirloom jacket which would go anywhere at any time of day.

'Try it on.' Marc took it from her and held it for her to slip her arms in the sleeves. 'Turn around. Yes, it's great on you...very becoming.'

'Do you realise what it would have cost?' Sophie's eyes rolled as she told him. 'It's totally over the top for a little help with her shopping.'

'She can't take it with her, Sophie,' was his dry response. 'It gives her a kick to play fairy godmother sometimes. Come here.' He drew her to him and, taking the ends of the scarf, tried tying it in different ways. 'When the wind comes slicing down from the Dolomites you'll be glad of this wrapped round your chin.'

'It's the most beautiful thing I've ever owned.' Underlying her delight in the jacket and her gratitude for Martha's generosity was the deep, secret pleasure of having him standing close and almost but not quite touching her.

He let the ends fall. 'There may be a note from Martha.' He rummaged through the tissue. 'No...not here. Feel in the pockets.'

She obeyed and produced a small envelope of the handmade marbled paper revived in Venice in the seventies. Inside was a card.

On it, the American had written, 'To keep you snug through the winter. You did so much to make my return to Venice enjoyable. Love, Martha.'

Sophie's throat closed up. She hung her head, embarrassed by the tears welling in her eyes.

'Hey...' Marc tipped up her chin. 'What did she say to make you weepy.'

'N-nothing.' Blinking hard, she gave him the card to distract him. 'It's just such a sweet thing to do...so incredibly generous,' she said huskily. Because she was knocked off balance, she added impulsively, 'Wouldn't it be lovely if Professor Grant turned out to be the third great love of her life?'

'It would be nice for them both to find a compatible companion. Being old can be lonely, even for people who have large families like Martha's. But as for falling in love...' He shrugged.

'I don't see why not,' said Sophie. 'If people have loving hearts, what has age got to do with it? Except, perhaps, sexually, and that's not the whole of love, is it?'

She was aware, as she said it, that she was speaking more freely than was wise. Her emotions were too close to the surface. She was liable to say something she might regret later.

'I'll put this away,' she said more briskly, taking off the jacket and folding it into the box.

When she returned from her room, Marc was behind his desk, staring into space in a manner unusual for him. As she was crossing the room he returned from wherever his thoughts had taken him.

'I expect you'll be writing to Martha,' he said. 'If you like, I'll take the letter with me when I go to New York on Thursday. It will get to her sooner than if you mail it from here.'

'Thank you. I'll write tonight.'

As they resumed work she wondered if he disagreed with her unguarded remark that sex was only part of love. Perhaps he didn't believe in love in her sense of the word.

During one of Marc's frequent absences, Sophie was walking away from one of the *vaporetto* stops when someone said in English, 'Excuse me, *signorina* ...'

Turning, she found a thin-faced young man smiling at her. His face seemed vaguely familiar.

'I was behind you when you bought your ticket. But you didn't have it franked by the machine. Perhaps, as a visitor to Venice, you don't realise it's necessary. There's a heavy fine for using the *vaporetti* with an unfranked ticket.'

Sophie fished in her pocket. 'Isn't the ticket dated?'

'Yes, but it still has to be franked. May I show you?'

He led her back to the walkway between the ticket office and the landing stage to show her what she should have done before boarding the *vaporetto* a few stops along the Grand Canal.

In the past Sophie had had no reason to use this form of transport, and latterly she and Paolo had walked everywhere.

'How stupid of me not to realise—'

The young man shook his head. 'Many visitors don't. Most of the ticket inspections are during the rush hour. The on-the-spot fines are high, to make it not worth the risk of travelling without a franked ticket, which, as you can see, is very easy to do.'

'How kind of you to tell me. Thank you. I feel we've met before, but I can't think where,' she said uncertainly.

'I work in my aunt's bookshop. You've been in the shop a couple of times.'

'Of course...I remember now. The last time I was there some people came in to ask the way. I thought it was very helpful of you to tell them in their own language. In your place I would have pretended not to understand. Their manner was anything but polite. They hadn't even mastered the Italian for thank you.'

'It doesn't happen often. You, I know, speak excellent Italian, and you've been in Venice longer than most of our visitors.'

'I'm working here.'

'Then I must introduce myself. I'm Damiano Fabbro.'
He offered a thin hand.

Sophie had no hesitation in telling him her name.
Instinct told her this wasn't a pick-up.

The day came when Marc said, 'You've been here a
month now, Sophie. I'm satisfied. Are you?'

'Very much so.'

'In that case the time has come for you to think about
somewhere else to live... somewhere you'll feel more at
home than a hotel room.'

'My room has a stupendous view. I'll never find a
better outlook than from the middle of the Riva across
the *bacino* to San Giorgio Maggiore.'

'Someone I know from Milan has a very small top-
floor *pied-à-terre* in a tall house on the Zattere. The
owner has gone to Rio for a couple of years and intended to put the flat in the hands of a letting agency.
However, on your behalf, I have first refusal. Shall we
go and look the place over?'

'Can you spare the time?'

'If I couldn't, I wouldn't have suggested it.' He was
always slightly caustic when people—others as well as
herself—made pointless statements or asked unnecessary questions. At first she had felt somewhat
crushed, but by now she had learnt to live with it and
even, sometimes, to riposte. As she did now.

'Actually that was a *politezza*.'

From cheekbone to chin, his tanned skin creased in a
smile.

'Do I browbeat you?'

'You can be a little... intimidating.'

'Sometimes it's necessary... but not, I admit, in your
case. You are driven by your own ambition, needing
neither carrot nor stick to make you do your best. Come
on; let's go.'

They went down the stairs at a run, as Marc and Chiara always did and as Sophie had learnt to.

As they left the *palazzo* and headed for the Zattere, the waterfront named after the rafts which had once been moored there, Marc said, 'My friend's flat has one major drawback as far as most people of middle age and older are concerned. To reach it one has to climb four flights of rather steep stairs. Otherwise it has every comfort— air-con for the summer heat, an excellent form of heating for the cold months ahead. It often surprises people to find it can snow here in winter. Last year one of the maids broke her arm slipping on a bridge. In icy conditions, the Three Graces don't venture out.'

It wasn't the first time he had referred in this way to his aunts. Although, whenever she had seen them together, Marc had been unfailingly courteous, she guessed that Constanzia, Caterina and Clara tried his patience. They meant well and doted on him, but they were often tactless and insatiably inquisitive. She could understand why he wanted a place of his own.

The front door of the flat was next to a *sotto-portego*—the Venetian name for a covered passageway.

'In New York or London an entrance with a dark alley beside it would be considered hazardous,' said Marc as he unlocked the door. 'But here that isn't a worry.'

He went ahead up the stairs, unlocking another door at the top of the final flight. The staircase, with its drab grey walls, was an unprepossessing approach to the eyrie at the top and Sophie couldn't help wondering if she wanted to lug heavy bags of household supplies and groceries up more than sixty stairs.

But when Marc opened the door and stood back for her to enter an unusually spacious living room, at present aglow with the first flush of sunset, she forgot the long haul to reach it.

The light was filtering through the gaps in wide rattan blinds. As he began to roll these up and fasten the cords to cleats like the ones on *Venezia* and other sailing vessels, she saw that to the south was the sun-gilded skyline of the Giudecca and in the opposite direction was a vista of Roman-tiled rooftops very similar to Marc's view from his desk.

He showed her the bedroom and bathroom. The kitchen was in a corner of the living area, concealed from the rest of the room by a bank of cupboards.

'What do you think?' he asked, after showing her around.

'I love it, but what's the rent?'

When Marc told her, she raised her eyebrows. 'Surely, even with those stairs, it's worth a lot more than that?'

He shrugged. 'I wouldn't know. I'm sure the agent has advised the owner of what the market will bear.'

'It's a snip. I'll take it,' she decided.

'Would you like to move in right away? How long will it take you to pack?'

'I haven't unpacked my big case—the one with my household goods, such as they are. Packing my clothes isn't a long job...not more than half an hour.'

'Right. You go back and do that and I'll come by with the launch about seven o'clock. By eight you can be installed.'

'It's a very kind offer but—'

'That's settled,' he cut in briskly, walking back to the door. 'I think you'll be comfortable here. It's rather sparsely furnished, but from your point of view that's better than being too cluttered. There's room for some personal touches. I'll be interested to see what sort of stamp you put on it.'

*   *   *

Sophie had settled her account with the hotel and was sitting in the lobby with her luggage beside her when Marc arrived promptly at seven.

He had not brought his boatman, she found when the hotel porter wheeled her luggage to the launch. At the other end, it was Marc who unloaded her bags, carried them to her front door and took them upstairs, without any sign that he wasn't accustomed to such labours or found them a test of his strength.

'While you were packing I organised a few basic supplies to keep you going overnight,' he said. 'Orange juice, bread, coffee and milk for breakfast... and for tonight some wine. Let's have a glass now, shall we? Then we'll go and eat at the Locanda Montin. It's only a stone's throw from here.'

'You're being terribly kind,' she said gratefully. 'I don't think many employers would go to these lengths to be helpful.'

'Let's forget that I'm your employer for this evening, shall we?'

She wasn't sure what he meant, but hesitated to ask him to be more specific.

Marc took a bottle of white wine out of the large refrigerator and opened a cupboard near it containing a variety of glasses.

'Why has your friend gone to Rio?' Sophie asked.

'One of the world's top cosmetic surgeons has a clinic there. Trina is also a surgeon. She's going to study his techniques and use them on patients in Italy. Cosmetic surgery has scarcely begun in Europe. In America face-lifts and "nips and tucks" are taken for granted. She wants to cash in on that here.'

When she made no comment, he said shrewdly, 'You don't approve?' And then, before she could answer, 'Neither do I, but when we've argued about it Trina has pointed out that *I'm* not devoting my life to a noble calling. Why should she?'

'You keep thousands of people in work. If that isn't a valuable function I don't know what is,' she said, with unintended vigour.

'Are you defending me, Sophie?' he asked, with a smile in his eyes.

'You don't need me to defend you,' she said, embarrassed.

'No... but I like it when you do.'

In the long pause that followed, Sophie was forced to acknowledge something she had been trying to deny. She was in love with him.

The walls of the Locanda Montin were hung almost frame to frame with paintings by many different artists. Most of the other diners were Italians, with only a sprinkling of foreigners at the pink-clothed tables with their homely rush-seated chairs.

As they were shown to a table by an elderly waiter with the air of a prince down on his luck, Sophie scanned the walls in search of a painting by Michael. Surely he must have come here long ago? But there was nothing she recognised.

While they ate Marc talked with unexpected seriousness about the future of the world and the best use of its resources. When he canvassed her views, Sophie found herself airing theories she had never shared with anyone before.

'You're even brighter than I thought when I took you on. How come you didn't go to college?' he asked.

Inwardly glowing with pleasure, she said, 'I needed to earn my living sooner rather than later. Unfortunately a degree no longer guarantees a problem-free future. Some students come out of college with a massive over-draft. I played safe and opted for office skills. They've served me pretty well. There are rafts of graduates who would envy me my job here.'

When their coffee was served he asked for the bill. 'I'd better not keep you out late. You still have to unpack.'

Sophie had decided that while he was walking her home through the quiet streets of a city not noted for its night-life she would tell him her history. But Marc had more to say on the topics they had talked about at dinner, and very soon they were outside her door, which he unlocked for her. Then, handing over the key and barely giving her time to thank him for dinner, he said goodnight and strode away.

It seemed a curiously brisk ending to an agreeable evening.

An hour later, Sophie climbed into her new bed. Above it, a large skylight had been inserted in the sloping ceiling of the bedroom.

Perhaps it was having the stars overhead, evoking nights in the past when Michael had taken her sailing through the constellations, explaining their magical names to her, that made her feel his presence as if he were in the room.

'I'm in love with Marc,' she said aloud. 'Don't tell me I'm mad. I know it. The odds against him loving me are a million to one. But...I can't help myself.'

How her grandfather might have responded, had he been alive to receive this anxious confession, was something she would never know. But she did know, from what he had told her about her parents and about his own marriage to one of the beautiful models he had drawn for *Vogue* magazine, that he had believed a loving and lifelong partnership between a man and a woman to be among life's best prizes. But one not awarded to more than a fraction of the people who hoped to win it.

Although, in a way, it was a relief to have confronted the way she felt about Marc, instead of continuing to pretend she wasn't in love with him, Sophie didn't feel inclined to take Damiano into her confidence.

The bookseller was in love with an American girl spending several months working at the Peggy Guggenheim Foundation. She hadn't left a boyfriend behind and was hoping to extend her stay in Venice. But Damiano felt he had little hope of persuading her to stay there permanently. She was only twenty and seemed set on a career in the art world.

'Twenty is very young for a serious involvement,' said Sophie, during one of her chats with him.

Mostly they talked about Venice. Damiano's knowledge of the city's history was extensive, and what he told her about Marc's ancestors was not reassuring. On his mother's side, he came from a long line of powerful, ruthless men who had been notorious for their cavalier treatment of the women who had fallen in love with them.

One evening she was in the bookshop, discussing the exploits of another of the great Venetian dynasties, when Marc himself walked in.

At the sight of her perched on a high stool behind the counter his mobile left eyebrow became an inverted tick.

His greeting included them both, but then, as if she had vanished—and she wished she could—he turned to Damiano to order some books he had seen reviewed in the *New York Herald Tribune*. As she already knew, he was an extravagant book-buyer, ordering expensive art books as casually as if they were bargains from the weekend stalls in the Campo San Stefano.

As he gave Damiano the details carried in his phenomenal memory he scanned the display on the counter, opening some of the covers to read what was written on the inside flaps of the jackets.

She feasted her eyes on his face, wishing she had the skill to reproduce his features on paper—the broad forehead defined by his thick black hair and straight eyebrows, the angular cheekbones and nose, the wide mouth and strong, square chin slightly dented at its centre. Although Michael could have drawn those features with a few expert strokes of charcoal on paper, Marc's face was actually more suited to the art of the sculptor.

She was thinking this when he looked up, and before she had time to switch her gaze elsewhere he caught it fixed on him and held it.

'What are you reading at the moment, Sophie?'

She told him the name of a novel recommended and lent to her by Damiano. Knowing she would return them to the shop in immaculate condition, he often insisted on lending her books he thought she would enjoy from his stock.

'I rarely read fiction,' said Marc. 'My aunts devour it like chocolate. I prefer to read about real lives.' He placed a couple of books on top of the till. 'I'll have these as well ... on my account, please.'

A few moments later he had gone, leaving her with the feeling that he disapproved of finding his personal assistant sitting in the shop as if she were Damiano's helper.

'We should miss his account if he took his custom elsewhere. He spends a lot of money with us,' said Damiano.

Sophie nodded. 'I know.' She glanced at her watch. 'I'd better be going. *Ciao* ...'

Outside the shop, she looked along the street in the direction Marc had taken. He was not in sight, but even his long stride could hardly have taken him as far as the end of it yet. He must be in one of the neighbouring shops.

Knowing she was behaving like a lovesick teenager, she sauntered past them at a leisurely pace, hoping he would emerge. On and off she had spent all day in his company, yet she longed for more. The evenings seemed endless intervals between the vital hours at the *palazzo*.

Outside two of the shops she loitered, gazing at the displays, hoping to see a tall reflection joining hers in the plate glass. But it didn't happen.

She walked home with the desolate knowledge that she was making a fool of herself, and that the pain and frustration of being in love with Marc Washington was going to get worse rather than better.

CHAPTER TWELVE

ON THE morning of her twenty-sixth birthday, feeling slightly cast down by the thought that in four years' time she would be thirty, Sophie walked into her office to find it full of flowers, with several gift-wrapped parcels lying on her desk.

Three were from Marc's aunts and one from Chiara. They could only have known it was her birthday because he had told them. The largest parcel had his signature on the tag and she left it unopened while she unwrapped the others.

Chiara had given her scent and the aunts' gifts were a pair of hand-embroidered pillowcases, a silk scarf and a leather-bound photograph album. Marc's parcel contained a de luxe volume on paintings of Venice by twentieth-century artists. It was one she had seen and coveted in Damiano's aunt's shop but had felt was outside her budget. Now it was hers, the lasting pleasure of its pages immeasurably enhanced by the simple inscription on the flyleaf, 'To Sophie from Marc,' and the date.

She was unable to thank him for it immediately because he had gone to Prague and was due back that afternoon. As the aunts were not early risers, she left it until mid-morning to go down and thank them and his cousin.

They insisted she lunch with them, and the chef produced a special pudding to mark the occasion. Sophie was touched by their kindness, but it was the fact that Marc had filed her birth date in his phenomenal memory which meant the most to her.

During the afternoon she received a message from the Prague office. Marc's return flight had been put back. But he had booked a table for dinner and would collect her from her flat at eight o'clock.

In Sophie's absence, the postman had delivered a large envelope with an array of United States stamps on it: a typically funny, flamboyant American birthday card chosen by Merle, with several one-line greetings from other friends.

It was nice that they had remembered her. Inevitably, birthdays were times when she was particularly conscious of having no family ties.

Not knowing where Marc was taking her or who else might be there made it difficult to know what to wear. After reviewing her wardrobe, she decided on the outfit she had worn in Paris, but with a shorter skirt than the one she had travelled in and a new pair of sheer black tights.

She was ready long before she needed to be and spent the interval restlessly pacing the living room, annoyed with herself for being as absurdly on edge as if it were her first date. She wasn't even sure that she would have Marc to herself. He might have invited others.

When the bell rang, she ran down the stairs to find Antonio, the boatman, waiting outside the street door. For an instant she felt cold panic, fearing an accident. Then he explained that the boss was running late and would meet her at the restaurant.

After taking her most of the way by water, Antonio insisted on escorting her to the door of the restaurant and handing her over to the head waiter, who showed her to a secluded corner table laid for two.

Less than five minutes later Marc arrived. 'Many happy returns,' he said as he joined her, only the dampness of his hair betraying that he had been rushed.

'Thank you...and thank you for your wonderful present. It's exactly what I would have chosen if I'd been offered the freedom of every shop in the city. Have you had a difficult day?'

He shrugged. 'It started badly, but—' he gave her a glinting smile '—all's well that ends well. Tell me about your day.'

The wine waiter had already brought champagne to the table and filled a glass for Sophie. So far she had only taken a couple of sips. Now he did the same for Marc who, as the bottle was returned to its bucket of ice, lifted his glass to her. 'To your twenty-seventh year. May it bring you a lot of things on your wish list.'

'Thank you.' This time she drank a mouthful of the chilled golden wine, knowing it would quickly enter her bloodstream, hoping it would give a sparkle to her conversation. She wanted to please and amuse him, but when she had told him about her other presents and the lunch party with his aunts she found herself strapped for subjects having nothing to do with their working life.

The only thing she could come up with was, 'You never finished telling me the story of the haunted mirror. I said that as ghost stories go it was rather a nice one. You said, "Actually, no." What did you mean?'

As she spoke she wondered if he would remember why he hadn't finished the story and felt sure he would.

'Apparently, when the princess and her lady-in-waiting compared notes, it was clear they had seen two separate pairs of lovers,' said Marc. 'We don't know who the princess saw. Since they were in bed, naked, there were no clues to the date of the time-warp she'd entered...if you believe in such things.'

'But you don't.'

'What makes you think that?' he asked.

'You believe in realities, not fantasies.'

'On the whole, yes,' he agreed. 'But at the beginning of this century supersonic flight was a fantasy. Now millions of ordinary people are surfing the internet from their living rooms. The future is full of things which seem impossible to us. As to the past...who knows? Perhaps it's still there, like a radio station we can't reach because we don't know the waveband. Anyway, what the lady-in-waiting tuned into wasn't the same channel as the princess had seen earlier that night. There were two different people making love by the light of candles, and then suddenly a dark shape...the silhouette of a man standing at the foot of the bed.'

Sophie drew in her breath.

'We have a letter in the archives in which she described what happened next,' Marc continued. 'Briefly, the intruder moved to one side, clearing her view of the lovers. They disengaged, looking alarmed. As well they might. What happened next was a blast from some sort of blunderbuss. The results were so gruesome, the lady-in-waiting fainted.'

Sophie's face must have reflected her feelings at seeing, in her imagination, the horror he hadn't described but which she could easily visualise.

Reaching across the table to cover her hand with his, Marc said, 'I shouldn't have told you.'

The intimate gesture sent a strange frisson through her. She said, 'No, no...it's interesting. Do the archives hold any evidence that such a thing might really have happened?'

'Plenty. It happened in the eighteenth century. The *marchese* of the time returned from an evening with his mistress to find his wife in bed with a handsome young servant. He must have suspected something to enter the bedroom armed. At the time morals in Venice were notoriously lax, but he must have been a jealous man who didn't subscribe to the view that an unfaithful husband gave his wife licence to do as she pleased.'

Marc's hand still lay on hers. He seemed to have forgotten it was there. But Sophie was sharply aware of his long fingers enfolding hers, sending a current of feeling to the top of her arm. She was both relieved and sorry when the arrival of their meal caused him to break the contact.

'Let's talk about something more appropriate to a birthday celebration. How did you celebrate last year?'

'I was sharing an apartment. My flatmate, Merle, laid on a party for me.'

'Do you miss that arrangement?'

Sophie shook her head. 'I might in another big city. But Venice has a villagey atmosphere.'

'Was the man of the moment at last year's party?'

'There was no man of the moment.'

'But there have been men in your life?'

'At twenty-six it would be rather extraordinary if I'd never thought myself in love.'

'Only thought?'

'If it had ever been the real thing, I shouldn't be here now, should I?'

'I suppose not. Are you still looking for the real thing?'

'Isn't everyone?'

'Are they?' He gave a slight shrug. 'I wouldn't have thought so. Money and power seem more popular objectives. They always were among men and now they're the principal goals of many of your sex. Women like Martha Henderson don't seem to exist any more.'

'She didn't have to work, and wouldn't have been encouraged to. Chiara's the first girl I've met who doesn't have a career, or even a time-filling job. When you have to compete in the rat race you develop a protective shell.'

She had meant to leave it at that, but then, on impulse, added, 'And women see through men more. Your

sex has lost its mystique. Women realise that not many
men come up to their expectations of what a man should
be like.'

'Speaking for yourself, what should a man be like?'

He asked with a gleam of amusement, making her feel
she was about to cross a conversational quagmire and
could quickly find herself floundering.

'Kind to women and children, fair in his dealings with
his own sex. Not a very tall order.'

'A generalisation. Be specific. What do *you* want from
a man? Surely more than kindness and fairness? If that's
all you want you could find yourself saddled with
dullness.'

'Naturally I want perfection,' she said, with a smile
and a gesture to show she was joking. 'The brave, gentle,
handsome knight of all the best fairy tales.'

'A tall order,' Marc said drily.

In response to his signal, the alert head waiter brought
menus. Looking for something light for dessert, Sophie
regretted her answer. Instead of sounding like a naïve
teenager, she should have said something witty.

Having entered the restaurant from the street, she expected to leave the same way. Instead, as they left their
table, the head waiter came forward, saying. 'If you will
follow me, *signorina* . . .'

Somewhat baffled, she obeyed and found herself being
led in a different direction, down some stairs and along
a passage which, when it turned a corner, brought them
to a doorway with a gondola moored outside it.

'It seemed an appropriate conclusion to your birthday,'
said Marc, when she turned to look up at him.

He said a smiling good evening to the gondolier, an
elderly man who had swept off his hat with a gallant
flourish when he saw Sophie.

The last thing she had expected was to find herself being handed into a gondola and, when she was seated on the cushioned sofa, having a rug draped over her legs by Marc.

'Although it's not cold tonight, it's always cooler on the water, and we're taking a roundabout route,' said Marc as he tucked it round her.

When he was seated beside her, another waiter appeared carrying a small wicker hamper. He gave it to the head waiter, who placed it where Marc could reach it before bidding them goodnight.

'The basket is an heirloom,' said Marc. 'I had it sent round earlier. It was fitted out for my maternal grandfather, who liked to take the air with his current mistress beside him. He would drink and smoke a cigar and she would eat Brussels chocolates. He had a theory that chocolate made women amorous, and he liked them generously curved. Tonight...it only contains a flask of freshly made coffee and a rather special liqueur brandy I think you'll like.'

The slight pause and the hint of devilment in his smile made Sophie wonder if he was merely teasing her, or if, in his experience, a smooth but potent liqueur was more effective than chocolates in making women responsive.

A further surprise was in store for her. As the gondola glided past the junction with another canal a second gondola came into view, and in it were seated three violinists who, as it moved into place behind theirs, began to play.

'Heavens! When you organise a treat, you really go to town,' she said, astonished that he should go to these lengths to please her.

'Why not?'

The response to that was, Why? But she didn't say it, or even allow her thoughts to linger on the reasons he might have. There were times in life when to capture the pleasure of the fleeting moment was more important than pondering the motive behind it or the possible outcome.

She leaned back against the cushions, enraptured by an experience she had often imagined but never expected to live.

By moonlight the city's waterways were at their most mysterious. She found herself seeing the Venice invisible from its bridges: tall, dark, forbidding façades relieved by elaborate windows, white marble friezes and balconies, and long-disused, barred water-gates, their steps thick with moss.

Behind them, the musicians were playing something by Vivaldi. Between them and the silver bow-prong stood a large basket filled with late-blooming roses from the *palazzo*'s sheltered garden, their sweetness wafting back like the breath of summer.

He had catered to every sense, she realised as he gave her a cup of coffee and placed a small crystal liqueur glass where she could reach it.

Every sense except touch.

Presently the lights of a restaurant, with diners sitting outside, changed the surface of the canal from silver and black to green and bronze.

'Let's not disappoint the romantics by sitting like strangers,' said Marc.

He lifted his arm and laid it along the cushions behind her shoulders. As the diners, alerted by the music, broke off their conversations to stare at the two gondolas, he took Sophie's hand and kissed it, not symbolically but with his lips touching her skin for two or three breath-stopping seconds.

From the tables behind the railing at the canal's edge came the momentary dazzle of an automatic flash as someone seized the chance to add another photo to their reel.

Someone else wanted one too. 'Do that again, would you, please?' The voice was male, the accent American.

Marc gave a smiling glance over his shoulder. 'No problem.' He repeated the gesture, this time holding her hand to his mouth rather longer.

Then the restaurant slid away behind them, the voices and laughter of its patrons lost in the sweeping strings of the violins.

Marc replaced her hand in her lap, but he didn't remove his arm from behind her. She wondered if, regardless of the gondolier, the next time they passed through a dark place he meant to kiss her properly and what she would do if he did.

Being kissed by her boss wasn't a dilemma she had had to deal with before. She had no idea how to handle it. Her common sense and her instincts were in diametric conflict. As a woman, she wanted to be kissed. As his personal assistant, she knew it could wreck their relationship and perhaps bring an end to her job here.

But Marc didn't kiss her. Gliding under the final bridge, the gondola came to the breeze-ruffled wider waterway between where she lived and the Giudecca opposite. It danced and swayed on the choppier surface and the gondolier changed his stroke with centuries-old expertise.

The music came to an end moments before they arrived at a landing not far from her door. Once ashore, Sophie thanked the violinists.

'That was beautiful . . . unforgettable. I'll remember it all my life,' she said in Italian.

Turning to thank Marc, she found him holding the **basket** of roses. 'I'll carry this upstairs for you, then **walk** back,' he said in English, before switching to **Italian** to add his thanks to the two gondoliers and **the** musicians.

As Sophie and he walked away, and the gondolas moved in the direction of another canal further along, the lead violinist began the opening bars of a modern love song, the other two joining in.

She stopped to wave them on their way. 'Was that prearranged?' she asked.

'Not by me. Perhaps it's their way of saying they don't often have someone as charming as you to serenade.'

Sophie received that in silence. A few yards away from her door, she said, 'I meant it when I said I would never forget their music, nor everything else about this evening. It's been a wonderful birthday. I don't know how to thank you.'

'Your company was my reward.'

Sophie fished for her key. Having found it, she said, 'I can manage the basket. Please don't bother to come up.'

'It's no bother, Sophie.'

The night he had shown her the flat he had gone up the stairs ahead of her, as mannerly men were supposed to. This time he let her go first. As they climbed the first flight she remembered the night they had spent in Paris and his schoolfriend Patrick saying to him, 'You can't turn in this early...not in Paris. Or maybe you can. Who wouldn't with legs like that pair going up the stairs ahead of him? I'll bet she has splendid boobs too...'

Did Marc also remember? Did he have it in mind to end the evening in the way Patrick had thought they were going to end it in Paris—in bed together? Had this whole lovely evening been an expensive prelude to a practised seduction?

In Paris, Patrick's assumption had filled her with indignant anger. But she hadn't known Marc then. Now she did. Now she loved and admired him. Now a night in his arms would be heaven.

But not if it were just a try-out. Or the start of a casual affair.

She went up the stairs much more slowly than she normally did, trying to stave off the moment when he would make his move and she would have to respond or rebuff him.

Would she be able to rebuff him when her senses were still alight from the expectation of being kissed in the gondola?

At the top of the staircase she unlocked the door between the landing and the living room and felt for the light switch. It was connected to a table lamp and a concealed uplighter in a corner of the little roof garden.

'How about some more coffee?' Marc suggested as he entered the room behind her.

She could have come out with the hackneyed excuse that she was tired and tomorrow was a busy day, which indeed it would be. But she put off the critical moment, knowing as she did it that she was weakening her defences.

'Of course . . . it won't take long. There's a very good percolator. Do the roses need a drink too? Did you have your aunts' permission to plunder their garden for me?'

He set the basket on the big table in the corner between the sitting area and the kitchen. 'They have their stems in water. The basket is metal-lined. Actually the garden is mine, although the aunts treat it as theirs. I'll be glad to have a garden I don't share with three old ladies. Are you interested in gardening, Sophie?'

His manner was reassuringly friendly. Perhaps, after all, he had nothing in mind but coffee and conversation. Perhaps kissing her hand had been merely some good-natured play-acting for the benefit of the tourists. She wished she knew where she stood with him.

'I think I could be,' she said. 'When I was at boarding-school, I made friends with an old man who worked part-time in the kitchen garden. His name was Jeremiah Jones. When he was twelve, and the house was privately owned, he started work as a garden boy. I loved listening to his stories. He died soon after I left. He—'

She broke off, not wanting to bore him with reminiscences of no interest to him. She felt she was talking too much—partly from nervous tension and partly, perhaps, from the effect of the liqueur which had tasted innocuously smooth but was probably far more potent than rougher spirits.

'How did you find out he'd died?'

'His daughter wrote to me...to stop me writing to Jem. It turned out she'd had to read my letters to him. He couldn't read or write. I think he was probably dyslexic, but in his day they didn't know about such things.'

'Were you unhappy at boarding-school?'

'A bit homesick at first. Who isn't? Later on I enjoyed it. Oh—'

Her exclamation was caused by his coming to where she was busy setting the coffee-tray and taking a carton of brown sugar crystals out of her hand.

'I don't take sugar and neither do you.' He replaced it in the cupboard above the worktops where it belonged. Then he put his arms lightly round her. 'I don't like to think of you being homesick.'

CHAPTER THIRTEEN

THEIR bodies were only inches apart. Sophie felt he must hear the violent thumping of her heart. She looked at the knot of his tie, slightly above her eye level, until by force of will Marc made her meet his eyes, before drawing her closer to kiss her.

It was eight years since her first kiss and many months since her last time in Robert's arms. Neither his nor any other kisses had prepared her for this embrace with the man she worked for, the man she loved.

After the first few moments when his lips were gentle, giving her time to resist, suddenly passion took over. He kissed her as if by right, holding her hard against his powerful body, taking confident possession of her mouth.

Sophie's response astonished her. As if it were the most natural thing in the world, she put her arms round his neck and surrendered herself without reservation.

When the telephone started ringing, the sound seemed to come from a long way away, recognisable but irrelevant. Her eyes closed, her body a turmoil of delicious sensations, she ignored it. But it wouldn't stop and leave them in peace. Eventually Marc raised his head.

'You'd better answer it,' he said huskily, putting her away from him. His dark eyes glittered with desire.

Dazed, she went to the end table where the interruption came from. Picking up the receiver, trying, reluctantly, to come down to earth, she said, *'Pronto.'*

'Is that you, Sophie? It's Merle.'

For a minute she couldn't think who Merle was. It was on the tip of her tongue to say, You have the wrong number, ring off and hurry back to where she belonged—in Marc's arms.

Then her mind made the connection. 'Oh... Merle... hello. How are you?'

'I'm fine. How are you? Happy birthday.'

'Thank you.'

'Did you get my card?'

'Yes, I did. It's a beauty. It came today... perfect timing. Thank you.'

'I have some exciting news. I've won a trip to Europe, to Courchevel 1850... it's a swish ski resort in France.'

'That's wonderful, Merle,' said Sophie, looking in the direction of the kitchen.

Marc was where she had left him, still standing with his back to her. She couldn't signal to him until he turned round.

'It would be if I could ski, or wanted to learn,' said Merle. 'But I'm trying to get it switched to somewhere I want to vacation... preferably Venice.'

'Can you do that?'

'Maybe not, but I'm working on it.'

As Merle started going into details of how she had won the prize Marc turned slowly round. Across the room their eyes met. It made Sophie feel weak at the knees just to look at him across five metres of carpet. She knew if he kissed her again, she would be lost.

He was coming towards her when the percolator went into its final spasm. He turned back to attend to it.

Merle was still explaining. Sophie sank down on the sofa. She felt weak with longing to let events take their course from those heavenly minutes in his arms. He had brought her alive in a way she had never experienced. Her whole body ached with a yearning for those feelings to come to a natural and satisfying conclusion under the window to the stars in the other room.

Merle had started to wind up her call. 'So I'll fax you as soon as it's settled. It's nice to hear your voice. I miss you.'

'I miss you too, Merle. It will be great if you can come to Venice. I'll look forward to showing it to you.'

Merle said goodbye and rang off. Preoccupied with her prize and the hope of changing its location, she had forgotten to ask how Sophie had celebrated this year.

Marc was still behind the bank of units screening, from where she was sitting, most of the kitchen area. She debated joining him there, then decided to stay where she was, leaving the initiative with him.

Now her intelligence was coming back into play, telling her she would be mad to be swept away by her instincts.

Marc came round the end of the screen. 'Sophie, I'm going to take a rain check on the coffee. That call reminded me of a couple I have to make before I turn in. I'll say goodnight. There's no need to come down with me. Give me the key to the bottom door. I'll lock it and put the key through the letter box.'

His tone was friendly but final. For reasons she couldn't begin to guess, he had made up his mind and that was that.

Torn between disappointment and relief, Sophie went to her bag and found her keyring. As she started to detach the key he wanted he said, 'Let me do that. You may break your nails.'

The touch of his fingers as he took the keys from her sent a frisson of erotic sensation quivering through her nervous system.

Perhaps the contact had a similar effect on him. She saw his jaw muscles tense.

Detaching the key, he gave the ring back to her, but in such a way that the contact wasn't repeated. 'I'll call you tomorrow. Goodnight.'

'Goodnight...and thank you again for a wonderful evening.'

He acknowledged her thanks with a nod and headed for the door.

When he had gone, closing the door to the stairway behind him, Sophie collapsed on the sofa, taking off her shoes before drawing her legs up beside her.

A horrible feeling of rejection was beginning to come over her. Why had Marc had second thoughts? She didn't believe his excuse that he had some calls to make.

It was true he was flying out tomorrow and wouldn't be back for several days, possibly a week. But if the calls were to local numbers on personal matters he would have made them earlier, before joining her at the restaurant. Everything outstanding in his official diary had been dealt with before she'd left the *palazzo*. The calls had been a pretext to get him out of the apartment. Why? What had changed him from the man who had kissed her with such intensity to the man who had said a courteous but distant goodnight?

The question was still tormenting her when she heard various church bells strike two and rose from her rumpled bed to make herself a cup of *camomilla*, hoping it would help her to sleep.

Merle and many of the people she had known in London and New York had routinely taken sleeping pills. But it was only since coming back to Venice that Sophie had found herself tossing and turning at night. She had never lost sleep over her relationship with Robert. But he hadn't made her feel the way Marc did. She had never shivered and burned with longing for him. She had never felt that if anything happened to him it would be the end of the world for her as well.

*   *   *

It was mid-afternoon the next day when Marc called her from Copenhagen, where he was attending a conference.

He sounded as if nothing had changed, yesterday had never happened and they were still on their previous footing. But she couldn't believe that their kisses had meant nothing to him. He had been as strongly aroused as she had, perhaps more so. The closeness of their embrace had given her unequivocal proof that it was not only she who had felt desire raging through her.

When she finished work, she found Paolo waiting for her outside the street door.

She hadn't seen him for some time and had concluded, with relief, that he was pursuing someone else. Perhaps he was here on his mother's behalf, the bearer of an invitation to some family celebration.

'Hello, Paolo. What brings you here?'

'I need to talk to you,' he said. 'You didn't tell me you had left the hotel.'

'I would have, if I had run into you. It was never my intention to stay there permanently, you know. It was only a temporary roost till I found a place of my own.'

'Where is your new place?'

'On the Zattere.'

He raised his eyebrows. 'Property there is expensive.'

'It's not a large place. I'm renting it while the owner is overseas.'

'Who's the owner... a friend of your boss?'

She nodded.

'That's what he told you anyway.'

'What do you mean?'

'Maybe he owns it himself. Maybe it's one of his love-nests. He has several, so I've heard.'

'Gossip!' was Sophie's succinct comment.

'Not all of it. I saw you with him last night. I thought you were going out with the guy from the bookshop?'

'We're friends. Damiano's in love with an American. I'm someone to talk to about her.'

'More fool him... and more fool you if you get involved with your boss.'

'I'm not involved,' she said, with partial truth.

'Oh, no? What were you doing in a gondola with him, then? Taking dictation? I'll bet!'

'If you must know, it was my birthday. He was merely being nice.'

'If you believe that, you'll believe anything.' Paolo retorted sarcastically. 'Or do you take me for a fool? If he didn't seduce you last night, it's only because he likes to play with his women like a cat with a mouse. Answer me this—when he left... if he left... did he shake hands or kiss you?'

'I don't think that's any of your business, Paolo.'

'He kissed you!' he said triumphantly. 'And today he's rubbing his hands because he knows he's got you right where he wants you, or as near as makes no difference. In a few hours' time he'll be ringing your bell with a big bunch of flowers in his hand, and while you're putting them in water he'll come up behind you and start to nibble your neck, and the next thing you know you'll be on your back and—'

Sophie cut short this forecast by using the book she was carrying to give him a thump in the ribs. He was too well-muscled for it to hurt him badly, but it made him yelp in surprise.

'That may be a method you've found effective, Paolo, but I don't want to hear about it. Your advice is unnecessary and your style of giving it offensive. If that's all you have to say, I'd prefer to walk home alone.'

She quickened her pace, hoping he wouldn't follow. His words had touched her on the raw because they expressed her own doubts and fears about Marc's intentions towards her.

'Sophie...don't lose your temper.' Paolo was at her heels as she ran up the steps of a small bridge.

It led to the mouth of an alley too narrow for people to pass without making room for each other. Halfway along it, silhouetted by the last of the afternoon sun, an elderly man with a stick was shuffling towards her. Politeness obliged her to wait for him, but the look she flashed Paolo was a warning not to persist.

'I'm sorry.' His tone was penitent. 'I didn't mean to offend you. I shouldn't have put it like that.'

'I accept your apology. Now let's drop it.'

Looking chastened, he stayed at her elbow while the old man came slowly towards them with short, tottering steps.

'Let me walk as far as your door with you. If Mamma finds out you've moved and I don't even know your address, she'll give me a thump to match this bruise,' Paolo said, rubbing his side.

'You've had worse,' she said unsympathetically, remembering more than one black eye acquired in his pugnacious boyhood. 'You can bring your mother to see my flat, if you like, but I won't show it to you today. I'm not in a sociable mood...but not because Marc's coming round. He's away in Denmark and from there he's flying to London.'

Paolo made no comment on this. It wasn't until they had emerged from the alley that he said, 'How's the work going on the island? Are the bureaucrats giving you a hard time?'

'No more than bureaucrats anywhere. They need the right approach.'

'And we all know what this is,' he said, with a knowing grin and a graphic twist of the wrist.

'You're too cynical. Not everyone is corrupt. I don't believe Marc would use bribes to achieve his objectives.'

There was no doubt in her mind that he was a man of integrity in his business dealings. It was only his attitude to women she wasn't sure about.

Echoing her thoughts, Paolo said, 'If he's spending a mint of his own money to improve state property, there's no reason for them to obstruct him. Listen, Sophie, don't get mad at me, but there's something I've got to tell you.'

'Something about Marc?'

He nodded, his expression troubled.

'If it's something unpleasant, I don't want to hear it, Paolo. I expect it's pure supposition.'

'No, no...this time it's fact. This is something I *know*.'

She wanted to close her ears, to refuse to listen. But curiosity won. Everything to do with Marc was of such compelling importance to her.

'Very well, then, tell me...but don't expect me to believe it.'

'I wish there was no need to tell you. When I thought he was just your boss, I kept my mouth shut. He's the father of Marina Guilio's eldest son. She used to be a housemaid at Palazzo Cassiano.'

Sophie averted her face, not wanting him to see how much this statement had hurt her. She knew Paolo wasn't malicious. As a boy he had never been spiteful or thoughtlessly cruel.

This wasn't a slanderous piece of gossip motivated by jealousy. It had to be true. And it had the same effect as the summons she'd once had to see the headmistress of her boarding-school. She had known before she'd reached Miss Wilkinson's study that there could be only one reason why she had been sent for. Michael had had another heart attack, as the doctors had warned him was likely. Now Paolo was breaking the news that another man she loved was not the wholly admirable person she wanted him to be.

'How do you know this, Paolo?'

'Maria's brother is a gondolier. I had something going with another of his sisters for a while. She told me about it. I've seen the boy. He's the spitting image of your boss.'

'Does Marc acknowledge the boy? Does he support them?' she asked in a low voice.

'I expect he's forgotten her by now. He knew she was pregnant. She told him. Most likely he told her that it was her problem. Luckily she had a nice steady fellow in love with her. By the time the baby arrived she was married to Sirio.'

'Does he know the boy isn't his?'

Paolo shrugged. 'I wouldn't know. All I do know is that your boss caused her a lot of grief, and she wasn't the only one he loved and left in the lurch. I wouldn't want to see the same thing happen to you. I expect you've got too much savvy to get yourself in the family way, but even smart girls get hurt in other ways.'

'When did this happen? How old were they?'

'Stefano, the boy, is sixteen. They live near Padova now, on the country estate of the family Sirio worked for when he lived in Venice. From what I hear, they have a good life over there. They've three other children. It's turned out well for Marina, but she might have had a bad time of it if Sirio hadn't been there to pick up the pieces.'

'If the boy is sixteen, Marc would have been nineteen when he was conceived. How old is the boy's mother now?'

'About thirty-five, I suppose.'

'If they live near Padova, how do you know the boy is like Marc to look at?'

'They came back to Venice for a family wedding a couple of years ago. At fourteen Stefano was as tall as me and still growing. He's bright too. They say he'll get to university. I wonder if he'll ever come face to face with his natural *papa*. It would be a shock for them both...and a worse shock if your boss has a wife by then and hasn't come clean about his past.'

'You talk as if he has children all over the place,' Sophie said, with a touch of anger. 'It's not a crime to father a child, Paolo. For all you know, you may have done it yourself.'

'Not me! I made certain of that,' he assured her. 'Girls may say they're taking precautions, but you can never be sure. Besides, there are other reasons for a fellow to be careful. Anyway, now you know that your boss isn't whiter than white I hope you'll watch your step with him.'

Their conversation left Sophie very dejected. She had never closed her mind to the fact that a man of thirty-six must have what Michael's generation referred to as 'a past'. She had one herself, of sorts. They were both grown-up people living in an era when human relationships were more open, honest and, in many cases, more transient than they had ever been before.

At school she had been surprised to discover that most of the girls in her form had two sets of parents, each pair composed of a divorced natural parent and a step-parent.

Perhaps, if her father and mother had lived, their youthful marriage would have fallen apart, although somehow she didn't think so. They had both been in love with the sea as well as with each other. A bond like that was hard to break.

When Michael had talked about them he had made her believe that she, too, would one day find her true love and be happy ever after. Life on board *Venezia*, without television or newspapers, had sheltered her from the disillusionments encountered later. The ideals implanted by Michael were still deeply embedded in her psyche, and the knowledge that Marc, having seduced a housemaid, had failed to shoulder his responsibility for the outcome did not equate with her concept of chivalrous behaviour.

She wished she could hear his side of the story. Perhaps there had been extenuating circumstances. But she couldn't ask about it, and meanwhile her opinion of him had been tarnished. It made her deeply unhappy.

When Sophie went to the airport to meet Rowena Wyatt, she already knew a great deal about the English garden designer Marc had chosen to plan the grounds round the house on the island.

At Sophie's request, her opposite number in London had supplied a folder of cuttings about her, mainly from glossy magazines which had interviewed the designer and photographed gardens created by her. However, all the photographs in the file had showed the thirty-five-year-old divorcee in working gear: jeans and a blue denim shirt with a man's panama hat worn at a rakish angle, or dungarees over a heavy sweater and a knitted ski hat in the photographs taken in winter.

Expecting a country person, Sophie was unprepared for a vision of sophisticated city elegance in an aubergine suit with a short skirt and perfectly matched opaque tights showing off very good legs. The colour was wonderful with the designer's dark red hair.

After Sophie had introduced herself, she said, 'Mr Washington would have come to meet you himself, but he's in Genoa today. He'll be back this evening. Did you have a comfortable flight?'

Mrs Wyatt said that she had, except that her suitcase was missing. She had already reported this to the airline's agent and seemed confident it would turn up before she needed its contents. She was clearly an experienced traveller, and not a person who fussed if things did not go to plan.

'How long have you been with Mr Washington?' she asked on the way to the waiting launch.

'Not very long. You haven't met him yet, I believe?'

'No, this job was fixed up through friends. A few years ago the husband of a girl I was at school with bought a villa on Cap Ferrat in the south of France. I tackled the garden for them. Later Marc Washington stayed there, liked it, and contacted Delia when he needed a landscape designer. That's the way it tends to work. Where did he find you?'

'In New York, but I'm English by birth.'

'I wouldn't have guessed it, even though you speak it perfectly. You're one of those people who might come from almost anywhere.'

'Have you been to Venice before, Mrs Wyatt?'

'Call me Rowena. Yes, a couple of times. Tell me about this island. I like to know other people's impressions before seeing a place for myself.'

'I think it's lovely because I like wild, lonely places.'

'Do you? How unexpected.'

'Why unexpected?' asked Sophie.

Rowena appraised her thoughtfully. 'You look so...urbane. Every hair in place, every detail immaculate.'

'The same could be said about you. You look rather different in your working clothes.'

Rowena laughed. 'You've been researching me, have you? I tried to do some homework on your boss, but apart from a few opinions on the social grapevine I couldn't find a thing about him. He keeps himself to himself.'

Sophie nodded. 'The garden he wants you to make for him will never be featured in any of the glossies. He dislikes publicity.'

'That doesn't matter,' said Rowena. 'The cachet of creating his garden will be enough for me. I'm told his house on Long Island is a dream of beauty. Have you been there?'

'No. I've only seen Palazzo Cassiano. By the way, there's a dinner party there tonight. If your luggage hasn't turned up, you may need to buy something suitable. Your travel insurance should cover any reasonable expenses.'

'The last time I came,' said Rowena, 'there was an irresistible shop in that street named after the uprising. They had lovely things in pleated silk and crushed panne velvet.'

'You must mean Venetia Studium in Via XXII Marzo. Their things are inspired by Fortuny's designs,' said Sophie. She knew the shop well, and admired its window displays every time she passed that way. But she doubted if the prices would be considered 'reasonable' by the people who ran insurance companies.

'That's the place,' said Rowena. 'Is it a big dinner party? Will it be very formal?'

'No—informal and only eight people. The architect and his wife and a few other people, including myself.'

She had been surprised at being included, and had assumed it was because one of the guests was an authority on the flora of the lagoon and his partner was away at the moment. If Chiara wasn't considered suitable, Sophie would have thought that Marc could have found someone other than herself to be a makeweight. But she was looking forward to it and had given a good deal of thought to what she should wear.

After seeing Rowena installed in the same hotel where Mrs Henderson had stayed, Sophie returned to her office and made a call to the flight agent to ensure that everything possible was being done to retrieve the designer's baggage.

*   *   *

She had been home to change, and was checking the arrangements in the smaller of the *palazzo*'s two dining rooms, when Marc appeared.

He was wearing a pale grey suit with a cream silk shirt and cream and pale blue silk tie. He smelt of bay rum and, as she caught the aroma, she had a crazy impulse to reach out and touch his jaw which sometimes, when he worked late, had darkened by this time of day.

Tonight, freshly shaved, it had the smooth sheen of bronze. He looked debonair, relaxed and compellingly attractive.

CHAPTER FOURTEEN

BEFORE inspecting the table, Marc looked at Sophie. She was wearing a black chiffon skirt over a scoop-necked black body and, over that, a long-sleeved cropped jacket of dark green silk velvet with cascades of tiny emerald-coloured beads in her ears.

'Pretty,' he said, touching one of them with a curled forefinger which didn't quite brush her cheek.

'Thank you,' she said briskly. 'Isn't the table beautiful?'

The centrepiece was an antique brass wine-cooler filled with lemons still with their dark green leaves. The golden sheen of the cooler was repeated in two large nautilus shells piled with walnuts. The wine glasses, hand-blown on Murano, had gilded rims.

While Marc was looking at the table he said, 'What do you make of Mrs Wyatt?'

'I like her. Unfortunately her suitcase went astray. It's been located but won't arrive till later. She's had to buy something to wear. She's been very calm about it.'

He gave her one of his penetrating looks. 'Would you tell me if you didn't like her?'

'Not at this stage. One has to spend more than half an hour with someone to have an opinion about them.'

'I had an opinion about you by the time we fastened our seat belts.'

'Really? What was it?'

Marc looked amused, but behind the amusement there was something else. 'That for a girl with such a kissable mouth you had a remarkably prim manner.'

Sophie leaned forward over the back of a chair to make a minute and unnecessary adjustment to one of the rat-tail forks already perfectly aligned by Domenico.

'Sometimes you make remarks some people would define as sexual harassment,' she said, in a low, tense voice.

'It's outside working hours, Sophie. Tonight you are one of my guests and I'll say what I please . . . within reason. I'm sure you're aware that you have an alluring mouth.'

'I've never been called prim before.'

'Perhaps you aren't . . . with other men. Perhaps it's only with me that you back off and put on your nun's face.'

Impulsively she said, 'It wasn't I who backed off the night you came back to my flat after my birthday dinner. It was you.'

'I can't deny that,' he agreed. 'But I wouldn't have done if the phone hadn't interrupted us. It gave me time to consider that perhaps later you might regret following things through to their natural conclusion. You'd had more to drink than usual. You were very re-laxed . . . perhaps not in total control.'

'How fortunate for me that *you* were,' she said, in a dulcet tone edged with more than a tinge of sarcasm, before turning to leave the room.

She was forced to stay by his fingers clamping her wrist. 'When you woke up the next day, did you still regret my not staying?'

'That's an arrogant assumption,' she said angrily. 'What makes you think I regretted it at all?'

'The fact that you've brought it up now.' As she opened her mouth to protest he continued, 'I regretted it. Why shouldn't you? Are you going to deny that you enjoyed kissing me? Come off it, Sophie. You came into my arms like a homing pigeon . . . and would have stayed there if the phone hadn't rung.'

'Another arrogant assumption. If you hadn't forestalled me, I should have asked you to leave.'

'Why?'

'Because to have allowed you to stay would have upset our working relationship. And apart from that I don't go in for casual sex.'

'I never supposed that you did. For all I know, you may never have made love with anyone. I think it's unlikely, but it's possible. If the will is strong and the flesh weak . . .' His other hand closed on her waist, drawing her towards him. 'But your fleshly urges aren't weak, are they, Sophie? When I had your mouth under mine I could have been kissing Veronica Franco.'

As he spoke he shifted his grip, his fingers sliding up from her wrist to enfold her hand, his thumb pressing into her palm in a way that sent shivers through her.

'She was our most famous courtesan,' Marc said in a low voice. 'A lady who knew a lot about pleasing men . . . as you do . . . when you let yourself go.'

Sophie felt her defences melting like butter in the sun. Surely he couldn't intend to kiss her again? Not here. Not now, with his guests expected at any moment.

If it had been his intention it was frustrated by Domenico, whose footsteps on the marble floor gave Marc time to release her and step back. When the butler appeared in the doorway, his employer had masked the expression which had been in his eyes seconds earlier.

When Domenico said good evening to him, he replied with his usual affability, and Sophie was able to escape and take refuge in another room, not in use this evening, where she wouldn't be disturbed and could recover her composure.

*   *   *

When Rowena arrived she was wearing a long fluid tunic of deep violet velvet, another colour which set off her fiery hair. She and Marc seemed to take to each other from the moment they shook hands.

At dinner she sat on his right, with the architect's wife on his left. The table was round, with the botanist seated directly opposite Marc with Sophie on his right.

Various delicious hot appetisers had been handed round in the drawing room beforehand and the main meal began with ravioli served in a hallowed-out pumpkin.

'For a new arrival in Venice, you ask most intelligent questions,' the botanist told Sophie while they were eating the main course, roast pheasant served on a bed of red pomegranate seeds.

'Which is no reason for you to monopolise her, Lorenzo,' said the man on her other side. 'It's my turn to bore this charming young lady who speaks our language with so little trace of accent.'

Although, in deference to Rowena, who had no Italian, those near her were speaking English, the botanist wasn't fluent, and had lapsed into his own language while conversing with Sophie.

'How does that come about?' her other neighbour enquired, as a rider to his smiling compliment.

Without going into details she didn't wish to disclose until she had come clean with Marc, it was an awkward question to answer. Glancing across the table, she became aware that he, too, was waiting for her reply.

She said lightly, 'I suppose I was born with a good ear for verbal sounds, the way some people have an ear for music.'

The meal concluded with one of the chef's specialities, a spectacular tart of figs glazed with blackcurrant liqueur syrup. Sophie had had it before and found it delicious, but tonight her enjoyment was marred by her awareness of what was happening on the opposite side of the table.

Marc and Rowena were hitting it off like two people made for each other. They were the right age, their heights matched; they harmonised in every way. The snatches of their conversation she was able to catch without losing track of what her neighbours were saying made it clear their rapport was more like that of old friends than new acquaintances.

Sophie had a sinking feeling that Rowena might be the woman Marc had been waiting for.

In the days that followed, Sophie suffered agonies of jealousy, an emotion she had always despised but was helpless to control when she saw the two of them together.

What surprised her was that she didn't dislike Rowena. She found her as attractive and amusing as Marc obviously did. Whatever the reason for the breakdown of the redhead's marriage, it was hard to see how Rowena could have been at fault. The more Sophie knew of her, the more she admired her.

A few days after Rowena's return to London, she faxed Sophie to say that a favourite bracelet was missing. She thought it might have come off while she was on the island. It was possible the clasp had broken. Could someone be sent to look for it? Although not intrinsically valuable, it had sentimental associations which meant a great deal to her.

Her message included a description and sketch. Sophie remembered seeing the bracelet on Rowena's left wrist, together with an unusual watch.

The fax was still in her hand when Marc walked into her office.

'You're frowning. What's the problem?'

'Rowena has mislaid a bracelet. She thinks it might be on the island. I was wondering how soon I could go over to look for it.'

'This afternoon. We'll both go.'

The snap decision startled her. 'Oh...I don't think you should waste your time. It may not be there. She could have lost it on her way back to England.'

'Possibly, but I don't remember seeing it the day she left. We were together that morning. Two pairs of eyes are better than one. We'll leave after lunch. Be at the water-gate at two.'

He went away, making her wonder why he had come in the first place. He wasn't a man who forgot what he was doing when some other matter cropped up.

She spent the rest of the morning in a tiswas about the afternoon. When he hadn't taken Rowena to the airport, she had realised there was nothing between them. She had misinterpreted the signals, as women were apt to do when they were in love with a man.

Now that Rowena had gone, Marc might intend to resume his pursuit of Sophie. There was no denying the current of tension between them. She felt it electrifying the atmosphere whenever they were together. She didn't trust herself to resist him if he took advantage of one of the island's secluded spots to make a determined pass at her.

The bright morning didn't last. By lunchtime the sky was cloudy. She had lunch at her desk instead of outside in the usually sheltered suntrap of the roof garden.

Afterwards she thought it advisable to dash back to the flat and change into trousers, a jersey and the warm but stylish jacket given her by Martha Henderson. It could be cold on the lagoon when the wind was in its present quarter.

She was at the water-gate ahead of time, surprised to see that, instead of the launch used for the airport run and the trip to Torcello, today a small speedboat was there. Luckily she had thought to bring a scarf. It was covering her hair and tied at the back of her neck by the time Marc joined her.

'Sensible girl!' he said approvingly, noticing how she was dressed. 'It could be a chilly trip. The launch is being serviced today, so we'll have to make do with this.' He stepped aboard and offered his hand to her.

There were speed limits on the canals, but out in the lagoon Sophie had often seen motorboats smashing through the water with their bows in the air and their sterns enveloped in spray.

Perhaps Marc might have driven like that in his salad days, but today he kept the speed moderate. Even so she was glad of her headscarf and sunglasses. The lenses protected her eyes from the chilly airstream slicing past the edges of the windscreen.

'Some women are chronic losers,' said Marc, breaking their silence. 'Gloves, sunglasses, umbrellas, earrings . . . I hope Rowena's not one of them.'

'I shouldn't think so. Anyone can lose a bracelet.'

'You don't wear them, I notice.'

'I've never had one as a present and I wouldn't buy one for myself. I prefer earrings and clips.'

'I must remember that at Christmas.'

'Do you normally give your PAs a present at Christmas?'

He slanted a mocking glance at her. 'If they've been good girls.'

How was she supposed to take that ambiguous answer?

Sophie averted her face, torn between her pleasure in his company and her dread that the attraction between them was building up to what one of her friends called 'the proposition point'. A point from which there would be two ways forward, but never any way back to the pre-proposition situation.

A spoonbill was passing overhead, a familiar sight to her once and now a nostalgic reminder of how much she loved this region and envied the man beside her his power to make himself part of it.

'I think we'll be looking for a needle in a haystack,' he said as they neared Capolavoro. 'Even the weather's against us. A sunny afternoon would have helped. In this light the gold parts won't shine. Anyway, we'll give it a go.'

They landed at a different place from where the barges would come with all the materials needed for the building of the house next spring. Their arrival disturbed various long-legged wading birds.

For the second time in an hour Sophie felt Marc's warm, strong grip enclosing her smaller hand as he helped her ashore. But he didn't prolong the contact.

'Rowena wandered all over the place the last time I came over with her. I suggest you go in that direction and I'll go in this.' He set off by the more overgrown of the diverging tracks.

As they moved away from each other Sophie forced herself to concentrate on the search for the few inches of metal which might perhaps be a souvenir of an equally fraught relationship in Rowena's past.

She had gone back to London with six rolls of exposed film in her hand luggage. It was possible that in order to capture a view from a better angle she had sometimes moved off the track. The chances of finding the bracelet if it had fallen in grass or low-growing scrub were very small—unless Marc was prepared to have someone go over the island, metre by metre, with a metal detector.

He might go to those lengths for a woman with whom he was having an affair, but Sophie no longer felt that he was interested in Rowena for reasons apart from her professional skills. If that had been the case, he would certainly have gone to the airport with her.

As she searched she was half-consciously aware of the familiar scents carried on the wind from the surrounding *barene*, the salt flats covered with marshy vegetation only covered at high tide.

The thought of the children who would grow up on the island—Marc's children—in more luxurious conditions but with the same surroundings she had grown up with, made her ache to tell him how much she loved him.

But how could she do that when she had no idea if his feelings for her went beyond mere physical attraction? If he had been an ordinary man she would have chanced it. But he was anything but ordinary. He was clever, good-looking and rich. He could take his pick. Why should he fall for someone who was neither beautiful, brilliant nor from his own milieu?

She was probing a clump of the sea lavender which, in late summer, coloured the islets with drifts of blue and pink, when a piercing whistle made her straighten. Looking round, she saw Marc waving to her. He was beyond shouting distance but near enough for her to see him point at the sky.

Looking up, Sophie saw that while her attention had been focused on the ground dark clouds had been approaching overhead. Not far away it was already raining. In ten minutes, or less, the first drops would fall on the island.

Marc was moving now, and pointing to a stone hut where they could shelter. He reached it ahead of her.

When she joined him, he said, 'I don't think it'll last long. Rain wasn't forecast this morning.'

Sophie hadn't much faith in forecasts. Like islanders the world over, she had grown up relying on experience rather than meteorology to tell her what the weather was going to do. To her eye, the approaching downpour looked likely to last some time.

There was nothing in the hut they could sit on. Marc was wearing a lightweight showerproof blouson over his cashmere sweater. He took it off, spread if on the tamped earth floor and sat down on it, leaving room for her to sit beside him.

Feeling that to remain standing would invite some sardonic comment, Sophie joined him. They sat side by side, each with one hand clasping the other wrist and their arms looped round their knees, watching the rain begin to beat down on the land outside the hut and the lagoon beyond it.

'Sorry about this. I guess coming over today wasn't such a good idea,' Marc said. She felt him looking at her.

'Your time is more valuable than mine. If I hadn't mentioned it to you, you wouldn't be stuck here. What I should have done, in retrospect, was to track down someone with a metal detector. I think that's the only hope of finding the bracelet.'

'You're probably right, but I wouldn't think metal detecting is as popular a hobby in Venice as it is in some other places. Perhaps we should tell Rowena to bring one with her next time. She who loses an object deserves the backache of finding it, as Confucius may well have said.'

'You don't have a bad back, do you?'

He shook his head. 'Do I look as if I might?'

'No, but I've known extremely fit-looking people who have to take care of their backs because of athletic injuries.'

She spoke with her eyes on the puddles starting to form in the sandy soil outside the shed. Superimposed on that image was another: the powerful wrists and sunburned hands alongside her own.

Her shoulder was less than an inch from the top of his arm, her foot in its navy deck shoe very close to his similar shoe and bare brown masculine ankle.

Every part of his body appealed to her in a way no other man's had. She had a crazy longing to be on a spacious rug with room to lie back and run her hand down his spine and say, Make love to me, Marc.

But she hadn't the nerve to do it. She wasn't that sort of woman. Her inhibitions insisted the first move must come from him.

'I was never into athletics or organised games,' said Marc. 'I prefer sports like skiing and climbing, things one can do on one's own. I also like games two can play.' He paused. 'Chess and backgammon.'

Sophie was sure he hadn't been thinking about board games in those few seconds of silence. Or was it only her own, overheated imagination which had instantly conjured up a vision of a king-size bed and Marc sitting on the side of it, beckoning her to him?

'I can't play either of them,' she said. 'Monopoly is my level.'

'I missed out on Monopoly. Didn't have that sort of childhood. I expect I'll get the hang of it when my children are the right age.'

She found it curiously painful to think of him, years hence, holding the bank of paper money for a family game. More than anything she wanted to share that future, to be the mother of the children shaking the dice-pot and exchanging gleeful looks when Dad was sent to jail or they cleaned him out in a property deal.

By now the lagoon was invisible, hidden by the curtain of water teeming down from a sky as unrelentingly dark as those she remembered from her first winter in England. It must have rained here as well but she had no memory of it. Her childhood had seemed a time of perpetual sunlight.

The cloudburst slackened eventually, but the rain didn't let up or show any sign of doing so. They must have been talking for an hour, one subject leading to another, when Marc said, 'I need to stretch,' and the next moment was on his feet, offering his hand to her.

Long ago, in her last year at school, she had known a boy who had taught her to clasp the wrist of someone offering a pull-up. She did this now and Marc's fingers closed round her forearm and drew her upright.

Still holding her, he said, 'It looks as if we may have to spend the night here.'

'I'd rather get drenched than do that.'

She only meant that a wetting seemed preferable to staying in a hut without the makings of a fire, a pile of sacks or any makeshift comforts.

His reaction was startling. About to let go, his fingers became a vice. His brows drew into a scowl she had never seen before.

'Damn you, Sophie, when are you going to start trusting me? If all I wanted was sex, I could have had you at your flat. You know that as well as I do, but you're still tensed up like a woman marooned with a crackpot. I've had enough.'

CHAPTER FIFTEEN

MARC let go of her arm, as if dropping something repugnant, and bent to snatch up his blouson, flapping it back and forth to dislodge the dirt it had picked up. His tan was suffused with the dark red of rage as he shrugged it on and fumbled to join up the zip, his fingers made clumsy by the force of his anger.

'Goddammit!' he said, through set teeth. Then the two sides fitted together and he yanked at the tag and gave her a last furious glare before heading for the doorway.

'Marc...wait...please don't leave me.'

The apprehension in her voice seemed to abate his anger.

'I didn't intend to,' he said curtly. 'There's a phone in the launch. I'm going to call for the covered launch to come and pick us up.'

She watched him run through the downpour. She was shivering, but not from cold. It was reaction to the flare-up between them.

When he came back his hair was plastered to his head, his clothes to his body, the drenched cloth defining every muscular contour of his tall, strong-boned frame. He was carrying a waterproof kitbag.

Raking his hair off his forehead, he said, 'Fortunately all the launches are equipped with emergency packs. There'll be a towel in here and a sweatshirt and pants. I'm going to strip off, but don't panic. I merely want to get out of these wet things and into something dry.'

Sophie averted her face but could not close her mind's eye to a vision of what was happening within a few feet of her: the powerful body being stripped of the sodden clothing and given a vigorous rub-down, making the tanned skin glow.

His voice broke into her thoughts. 'How could you think I would leave you alone here?'

'I—I thought you were angry... that you wanted to punish me.'

At first he didn't reply. She could hear the friction of the towel and guessed he was drying his back.

'Your safety and comfort are very important to me, Sophie,' he said, in an oddly gruff voice. 'I was a fool to lose track of you.'

'Lose track of me... what do you mean?'

'Are you going to go on pretending you don't know we've met before?'

Her head swung round to face him, but she was too startled by what he had said to notice that he was naked. 'I didn't know *you* knew that.'

Marc wrapped the towel unhurriedly round his hips. 'I knew when you came to be interviewed that I recognised something about you, but I didn't know why. I didn't discover the reason until we had lunch on Torcello with Martha Henderson. We passed the place where your grandfather's boat had been moored and it all slotted into place. You were that funny child grown-up... grown very beautiful.' The way he said it made her heart lurch. 'Why didn't you tell me? Why did you keep it a secret?'

'I don't know,' she answered quietly. 'I suppose I kept putting it off in case it put *you* off. We weren't what you'd call respectable, Michael and I. To someone like you we must have seemed almost vagrants.'

'I did think there was a danger of you ending up on the streets if the old man died and left you unprotected. That worried him too. He told me so. There was no one else he could tell. Fortunately, having come into my inheritance, I was in a position to do something about it. The money to finance your schooling and keep the old man in comfort for the few years left to him was a drop in the ocean of my grandfather's fortune.'

'*You* paid my school fees? But Michael said it was a legacy.'

'A windfall,' Marc said drily. 'A quixotic gesture I didn't follow through because that would have been too much trouble. It didn't involve any effort to transfer some funds to a bank account in his name. To keep an eye on you afterwards was too much bother. It's a selfish age, twenty-two. Perhaps it was just as well you were only eleven. If you'd been seventeen, I might have seduced you myself. I had no morals to speak of.'

'I don't believe that,' she said. 'You saved Michael's life. You knew the right thing to do. You came to the hospital afterwards. He thought you a fine young man.'

'He didn't know me long enough to see behind the facade. I haven't deceived you, have I? You've never trusted me.' He thrust his arms through the sleeves of a scarlet sweatshirt and pulled it over his head.

With his black hair damp and dishevelled, he looked younger and somehow less formidable. Or was that because he was revealing a side of himself she had never seen before?

She decided to tell him the truth. 'It's not a trustful situation...falling in love with someone so different from yourself that there doesn't seem to be any possible future in it.'

Marc pulled the sweatshirt down over his ribs. It was stretched by the breadth of his shoulders and inches too short in the arms.

'Are you telling me you love me?'

'I've tried not to but I can't help it. If you want me, I'm yours. I know it may end in tears, but it will be lovely while it lasts.'

'What are you proposing? That we live together?'

'That's what most people do.'

'We aren't "most people". You and I make our own rules. I want you to be my woman, my friend, my companion for the rest of my life. In my book that means being my wife—with no conditions, no safeguards, only total commitment to a lifetime of happiness.'

Sophie's eyes filled with tears. 'Oh, Marc... are you really saying this or am I dreaming?'

He came to where she was standing and put his arms lightly round her. 'I've wanted to tell you many times, but the moment was never quite right. The night of your birthday was the nearest I came to it. If it hadn't been for your friend ringing up from New York... As soon as you put the phone down I could see you were backing off—afraid I would take advantage of what your body wanted but your mind had begun to deny.'

He brought a hand up to her cheek, stroking it lightly with the back of his knuckles. 'Leaving you... saying goodnight... was the hardest thing I've ever had to do. But I knew if I went ahead it might be the first and last time for us. In the morning you'd feel I'd coerced you.'

Her feelings no longer masked, Sophie said softly, 'You coerce me every time you look at me. Something inside me melts. I'm no longer in charge of myself. It's a frightening feeling when you aren't sure the other person feels the same way.'

'I felt this way before you did... when it was still a mystery why you seemed so familiar. To love a woman before I knew her properly went against all my instincts. I'd seen too many disasters resulting from "love at first sight". The world is littered with failed relationships based on that fatal premise...'

His fingers caressed her neck, sliding upwards into her hair as he bent his head to kiss her.

The difference between this kiss and the kisses exchanged at her flat was that now her mind could surrender as eagerly as her body. She slipped her arms round his neck, delighting in the strength of the arms holding her close, the wide shoulders forming a shield between her and the world.

His ears were the first to catch the distant drone of an engine. Bringing their kisses to a reluctant conclusion, he said huskily, 'This isn't the time or the place anyway. One day this will be our home and we'll make love here many times. But tonight we'll find somewhere else...' His eyes smiled into hers. 'Somewhere a little more comfortable.'

Sophie had stopped pretending. She said, 'After you've picked up some dry clothes, you could come to my place.'

'"Two souls with but a single thought, two hearts that beat as one." Meanwhile I'd better put some pants on.'

Like the sweatshirt, the black sports pants were not a good fit, being too large at the waist and too short in the leg. But Marc had the physique and presence to carry off any clothing. It crossed her mind that when Carnival came he would look magnificent in the black tricorne hat and silk cloak, as worn by his mother's ancestors. Until now she hadn't been certain she would be here for Carnival. But now the future, this morning an unknown territory, had changed to a clearly marked map of a golden world they would journey through together.

The boatman who came for them brought an umbrella for himself and two more for them.

Marc said, 'One is enough.' And when he had opened it he drew her into its shelter with an arm round her waist. Aboard the launch, he kept her in the circle of his arm.

'What will your aunts say?' she said as the boat moved away from the landing stage. 'I'm sure they'll think me most unsuitable.'

'They'll think me far luckier than I deserve to be. They like everything about you.'

'They don't know everything about me. When they find out I'm the granddaughter of the old man who used to draw tourists on the Riva...'

'I had the impression he was someone rather special...perhaps an important artist before he lost his arm.'

Sophie explained about Michael's career in the fashion world. 'But not many people appreciate what wonderful draughtsmen the great fashion artists were.'

When they were nearly back to Venice, Marc instructed the boatman to take them to Sophie's flat rather than the *palazzo*.

'There is something I have to tell you before we announce our engagement,' he said. 'Something discreditable about me.'

'There's nothing you can tell me that would change the way I feel.'

'I hope not,' he said gravely. 'But I'm afraid it may hurt you.'

She was tempted to tell him she already knew but decided against it. Paolo's version of the story might be a long way from the truth.

In her flat, Sophie made instant coffee and asked him to pour out two brandies. When she sat down on the sofa Marc joined her there, but leaving a space between them.

'When I was eighteen,' he said, 'I thought myself in love with a beautiful girl called Marina, who worked for us as a maid. She was a little older—twenty—and she seemed to feel the same way. It wasn't difficult for us to find times and places to be alone together and the inevitable happened. We became lovers. I wanted to marry her but she felt, rightly as it turned out, that my family wouldn't consent. I couldn't touch my trust fund until I was twenty-one so we wouldn't have any money. Well, that was OK. We had all our lives ahead. We could wait a few years. Then Marina started a baby and marriage became more urgent.'

He paused, his expression withdrawn. Watching his face, Sophie knew in her bones that he had really loved the girl and hadn't been merely using her.

'When I talked to my grandfather,' said Marc, 'he wouldn't hear of our marrying. He said we were both far too young and unsuited in every way. There was a ferocious row and I told him to go to hell. But Marina wouldn't come away with me. She didn't want to leave her family and she didn't think I could earn a living for us without my family behind me. I still think she was wrong. I could have made it on my own.'

'I'm sure you could,' said Sophie.

That brought a slight smile to his face. 'Marina didn't have your adventurous spirit. She hadn't grown up on a boat under the aegis of an artist. Had I been more mature, I should have realised it was expecting too much for a girl from her close family background to run off with a guy like me. When it comes to the crunch, there aren't many women who are prepared to risk everything for love. Risk is not what your sex is about. Women are programmed to nest, not to take chances.'

Generally speaking, she agreed with him, and this wasn't the moment to say that she had different priorities.

'What happened?'

'My grandfather offered her a substantial lump sum and a long-term income for the child providing she agreed to have nothing more to do with me.'

Sophie gave an exclamation of distress. 'That was a cruel thing to do.'

'Some people would think it was generous. He thought it fair. In retrospect, I believe it was. Being older and wiser than I, he saw that a marriage between us would have been a disaster—like my parents' marriage. The reasons would have been different, but the outcome would have been the same. If Marina had loved me she would have refused his offer and come away with me.'

'Perhaps she did love you but knew that she wasn't right for you. Perhaps her parents pressured her into agreeing.'

'I'm sure they did, but I don't think they had to press hard. If a woman loves a man, she doesn't go and marry someone else a few weeks later.'

'Surely she might if she had a baby to consider?' But even as she said it Sophie knew that, loving Marc, she could never marry anyone else. To let another man make love to her would be unthinkable.

'That premise might have held water thirty or forty years ago,' said Marc. 'It doesn't today. Italy has its quota of single mothers like everywhere else. I suspect Marina's heart healed a lot faster than mine. I already knew that my mother had taken ruthless advantage of my father's passion for her. Marina's behaviour confirmed that women were devious creatures, not to be trusted. That remained my opinion until I met you. Almost immediately I fell in love with you. In fact I was pretty far gone by the end of our first evening together, in Paris. But when I realised who you were and that, for whatever reason, you weren't being straight with me, it revived my distrust of women.'

'I was on the point of telling you lots of times. One of the reasons I didn't was because of something that happened when I was a child. For a little while I went to school here. Only for a couple of months, and then Michael decided I wasn't being taught anything I couldn't learn from him and that I was being fed ideas he didn't approve of. The only thing I remember is being invited to another child's birthday party. I'd never been to a party so I was very excited.'

'How old were you when this happened?'

'About seven. Old enough to be worried about fitting in. I had a uniform dress to wear for school, but I didn't have any other dresses. I always wore shorts in summer and jeans in winter. So I went in clean jeans and a red jumper a lady on Burano had knitted for me. Michael had bought a red ribbon to thread through my plait. I must have looked quite nice.'

'I'm sure you looked adorable,' said Marc. 'But I suppose all the other little girls had expensive party dresses.'

'Yes, but that wasn't what hurt. The mother who was giving the party knew who I was and so did one of the other mothers. They had a whispered conversation and finally my hostess came over and led me out of the room. She said she was very sorry but I'd been invited by mistake and one of her maids would take me back to my grandfather. She gave me a big gift-wrapped parcel by way of compensation. But I never knew what was in it because Michael sent it back. I'd never seen him so angry. I was terrified he was going to go back there and storm at them.'

While Marc had been listening to this, his own expression had become increasingly thunderous. 'I'd like to know who it was who objected to you. She must have been a prize bitch,' he said. 'I don't think much of your hostess, but perhaps the other one's husband was her husband's boss—she may have been afraid to remind her whose house it was. I know there are people in Venice who worship money and status. There are people like that everywhere. But to humiliate a child...' His dark eyes were brilliant with anger.

'I don't think I felt humiliated, just baffled,' said Sophie. 'When he'd calmed down, Michael explained it to me. He said people like that didn't matter. They had different values and they were never happy. But the next day at school a lot of the girls weren't as friendly as before. One of them even parroted something said by her parents...that Michael was a down-and-out and the school shouldn't have accepted me as a pupil.'

'Surely you can't have thought I would look down on you?'

'No, but I felt your family might. I've learnt to conform to conventional society, but deep down inside I still feel I'm an outsider. Don't misunderstand me; I don't feel in any way inferior, just different. An alien being in a world where I have to survive but which often I don't like. Aliens shrink from revealing themselves,' she added, with a wry smile.

'We'll make our own world on Capolavoro,' said Marc. 'It will be even better than growing up on Torcello. I'll still have to go away sometimes, but not as often. I'm tired of jetting around from big city to big city. I want to live quietly with you and try to make up for the pain you must have felt after your grandfather died and left you alone in the world.'

'Perhaps we'll be even happier because we've both been through bad times,' Sophie said softly.

As she spoke, all over Venice bells started chiming the hour. She stood up and held out her hand to him. Marc took it and rose to his feet, his expression questioning.

'Last time you were here it was different. You thought you might be coercing me and I didn't know where I stood with you. This time there are no obstacles. Before we go back and break the news to your aunts, could we unplug the telephone and pick up where we left off?'

He scooped her up and, cradling her in strong arms, carried her towards the bedroom.

The next time the bells chimed the hour, Sophie opened her eyes to see that the sky had cleared and the rose-gold glow of a Venetian sunset was pouring through the skylight. Turning her head a little, she looked into smiling dark eyes and gave a long sigh of happiness.

At last she had found where she belonged.

AUTHOR'S NOTE

'WHERE do you get your ideas?'

Every professional writer has been asked that question many times.

I find my ideas while travelling. One lovely October day I was on the island of Torcello, waiting for the ferry, when I noticed an old boat moored a little way along the tow-path. The sea is in my blood and I've written more than twenty books with part of the action taking place on board a schooner or some other sailing boat. On the way back to Venice I wondered why anyone would leave a boat to rot at her moorings.

Later, missing my husband, who was far away in the foothills of the world's highest mountain, I sat in a *caffè* on the Riva, with a notebook on my lap and a pre-dinner *spritz* at my elbow. As I watched the sunset I found the story you have just read beginning to form in my mind.

Of all the places I've been to since my first trip abroad, none has cast such a strong spell on me as Venice. It deserves a place on everyone's travel wish list. I shall go again, as soon as possible, knowing there are other tales of the Venetian lagoon waiting to be written.

Anne Weale

MILLS & BOON®

Next Month's Romances

Each month you can choose from a wide variety of romance novels from Mills & Boon. Below are the new titles to look out for next month from the Presents and Enchanted series.

Presents™

JACK'S BABY	Emma Darcy
A MARRYING MAN?	Lindsay Armstrong
ULTIMATE TEMPTATION	Sara Craven
THE PRICE OF A WIFE	Helen Brooks
GETTING EVEN	Sharon Kendrick
TEMPTING LUCAS	Catherine Spencer
MAN TROUBLE!	Natalie Fox
A FORGOTTEN MAGIC	Kathleen O'Brien

Enchanted™

HUSBANDS ON HORSEBACK	
	Margaret Way & Diana Palmer
MACBRIDE'S DAUGHTER	Patricia Wilson
MARRYING THE BOSS!	Leigh Michaels
THE DADDY PROJECT	Suzanne Carey
BEHAVING BADLY!	Emma Richmond
A DOUBLE WEDDING	Patricia Knoll
TAKEOVER ENGAGEMENT	Elizabeth Duke
HUSBAND-TO-BE	Linda Miles

'Happy' Greetings!

Would you like to win a year's supply of Mills & Boon® books? Well you can and they're free! Simply complete the competition below and send it to us by 31st August 1997. The first five correct entries picked after the closing date will each win a year's subscription to the Mills & Boon series of their choice. What could be easier?

ACSPPMTHYHARSI

_ _ _ _ _ _   _ _ _ _ _ _ _

TPHEEYPSARA

 _ _ _ _ _   _ _ _ _ _ _

RAHIHPYBDYTAP

_ _ _ _ _   _ _ _ _ _ _ _

NHMYRTSPAAPNERUY

_ _ _ _ _   _ _ _ _ _   _ _ _ _ _ _

DYVLTEPYAANINSEPAH

_ _ _ _ _ _ _   _ _ _ _   _ _ _ _ _ _ _

YAYPNAHPEREW

 _ _ _ _ _   _ _ _ _ _ _

DMHPYAHRYOSETPA

_ _ _ _ _ _   _ _ _ _ _ _ _ _ _

VRHYPNARSAEYNPIA

_ _ _ _ _ _   _ _ _ _ _ _ _ _ _

Please turn over for details of how to enter ☞

How to enter...

There are eight jumbled up greetings overleaf, most of which you will probably hear at some point throughout the year. Each of the greetings is a 'happy' one, i.e. the word 'happy' is somewhere within it. All you have to do is identify each greeting and write your answers in the spaces provided. Good luck!

When you have unravelled each greeting don't forget to fill in your name and address in the space provided and tick the Mills & Boon® series you would like to receive if you are a winner. Then simply pop this page into an envelope (you don't even need a stamp) and post it today. Hurry—competition ends 31st August 1997.